# Mallory Hates Boys (and Gym)

# Mallory Hates Boys (and Gym)
## Ann M. Martin

AN
**APPLE**
PAPERBACK

SCHOLASTIC INC.
New York Toronto London Auckland Sydney

Cover art by Hodges Soileau

ISBN 0-590-45660-1

12 11 10 9 8 7 6 5 4 3 2 1                    2 3 4 5 6 7/9

Printed in the U.S.A.                                    40

First Scholastic printing, November 1992

*The author gratefully acknowledges*
*Suzanne Weyn*
*for her help in*
*preparing this manuscript.*

# Mallory Hates Boys (and Gym)

# CHAPTER 1

"Pandemonium!" I cried as I stepped into our rec room. "Utter pandemonium!"

None of my brothers and sisters even turned around. They were all too busy creating pandemonium.

*Pandemonium* was a new word in the vocabulary builder section of my English textbook. We'd just learned it in class that afternoon. The minute I saw the word, I knew it was one I'd have many chances to use. (I love it when I find a really great new word.) Pandemonium means: wild uproar and noise.

That's the Pike house, all right! Uproar and noise. I'm used to that, though. I don't have much choice since I have seven younger brothers and sisters. In fact, "uproar and noise" is the general state of things on most days.

Today was no different than usual. I was the last one home from school, and the kids were spread all over the rec room. Vanessa was lying on the rug watching a rock video. Claire had strewn pieces of her picture puzzle across the floor. Margo was loudly practicing a cheerleading cheer (even though she is not a cheerleader). The triplets were having a game of monkey-in-the-middle with a small orange Nerf ball. And Nicky was making weird noises with a speaker he'd just bought. (The speaker has three settings: loud, robot voice, and baby voice. When you speak into it, the speaker changes your voice any way you want. It's actually kind of cool.)

"This place is complete pandemonium!" I repeated, mostly because no one had paid any attention to me the first time.

"A panda?" inquired five-year-old Claire, looking up from her puzzle.

"No, not a panda. Pandemonium," I told her as I wiggled out of my backpack. "It means — "

"It sounds like a sickness," eight-year-old Nicky chimed in, putting down his speaker. He clutched his throat and bulged his eyes. "Help! I've got pandemonium. Call a doctor!" He spun around the room a few times before flinging himself on the floor.

"Very funny," I said, smiling despite my efforts to look unamused.

Vanessa, who is nine, glanced away from her video. "I think pandemonium sounds more like something you clean pans with."

She rolled onto her back and held up her hands. "I no longer have rough, dry hands because now I clean my dishes with *Pannnnn-demonium!*" she said, as if she were an actress on a commercial.

"No, it's not dishwashing stuff." I laughed. "Pandemonium means — hey!" The Nerf ball had bounced off my forehead. "Watch it! You're not supposed to be playing ball inside, anyway." I picked up the small, spongy ball which had dropped to my feet and squished it into the pocket of my jeans.

"Aw, come on, give it back," said Adam, annoyed. He's one of the identical triplets, who are ten.

"It's just a Nerf ball. It's not going to hurt anything." Jordan backed up Adam. (As usual.)

Byron didn't look like he minded, though. I think he was relieved not to be the monkey-in-the-middle anymore. He's not as athletic as Adam and Jordan. When he's the one trying to get the ball away, he can get stuck as the monkey for a long time.

Some people have trouble telling Byron, Adam, and Jordan apart. But to me, they are each so different that I never have a problem. I could pick Byron out just from the way he slouches. Besides, they don't dress alike. I'm always surprised when people confuse them.

At that moment, my mother came downstairs from the kitchen. "Hey! Hey! What is all this?" she scolded mildly. "Vanessa, turn off that TV. And did I hear something about a ball in the house?" The triplets' guilty expressions gave them away. "Well, take it ouside. Margo, you can do your cheering outside, too. It's a gorgeous day."

"We-must-go-outside. We-must-go-outside," Nicky chanted with his speaker set to robot-voice as he moved mechanically out of the rec room.

"Claire, pick up those puzzle pieces, please," Mom requested. Then she looked at me. The moment she did, I knew what was coming. I was tipped off by the way she glanced quickly at Claire before she spoke.

"Mallory," Mom said, "could you please watch Claire for a little while?" Just as I'd expected.

Don't get me wrong. I *love* to baby-sit. I love it so much that I'm even a member of a club called the Baby-sitters Club (which I'll tell you about later). But one thing I don't like about being the oldest of eight kids is that I'm *always* being asked to take care of one or more of them. (The other thing I don't like is the privacy problem. There's practically no privacy in my house.)

Sometimes Mom and Dad ask me to baby-sit when it's not convenient; like when I want to read, or write in my journal, or just be alone. When I go on a baby-sitting job for the BSC (Baby-sitters Club) I know exactly when and where I'll be sitting. (The club is super organized.) But at home, baby-sitting assignments can pop up unexpectedly.

Most of the time I just sigh and say okay. (Or smile and say okay, depending on my mood.) But today I really couldn't do it.

"I would, Mom, but Ben is coming over," I told her. "We're going to do our homework together."

Mom opened her mouth as if she were about to argue with me, but then she seemed to change her mind. "Okay," she said, kneeling and tossing the last of the puzzle pieces in the box. "I just wanted to make some phone calls. I can make them after supper."

"I'll watch Claire after supper," I offered.

Mom smiled. "It's a deal."

When Mom and Claire went outside, I was alone in the rec room. The clock on the wall said 3:15. "Oh, no!" I cried. Ben was coming over at 3:30. That left only fifteen minutes for me to get ready.

I raced up the stairs and into the room I share with Vanessa. "I have to get ready," I panted. Only I wasn't sure what I was supposed to do. I mean, it wasn't like I could take off my braces and my glasses. The braces are on for at least another year. (Thankfully, they're the clear plastic kind. I still hate them, though.) And I can't see without my glasses. I have begged — *begged* — my parents for contacts, but they say I'm too young. That makes no sense to me. An eleven-year-old is plenty old enough to take care of a pair of contact lenses. At least this eleven-year-old is.

It wasn't as if I could do anything with my hair, either. My longish red hair is curly and does whatever *it* wants — not what I tell it to.

And then there's my nose. All my relatives say I got it from my grandfather. Well, if it were up to me, he could have it back!

Just about the only thing I could change was my shirt. So I did. And my jeans, too, for the heck of it.

I looked at myself in the mirror and sighed hopelessly. I don't consider myself very pretty. But it never used to matter to me. Then I met Ben Hobart.

All of a sudden, for the first time in my life, I wished I were gorgeous. But to my surprise, Ben seems to like me just the way I am. (Talk about a lucky break! Then again, Ben isn't shallow, like some boys who only care about looks.)

Liking a guy is so weird. There's just no way to explain why suddenly you're so crazy about someone. By movie-star standards, Ben isn't a hunk or anything. (Even though I think he's totally adorable.) He has reddish-blond hair, sort of a round face, and freckles. He's tall. And he wears glasses. (Which makes me feel less self-conscious about my glasses.) Oh, and there's one thing that's very cool about Ben. His accent. His family is from Australia. When the Hobarts first moved to Stoneybrook, Connecticut (that's my town), some of the kids in school made fun of Ben's accent. I'm sure they were just jealous. Now everyone is used to it and no one teases him anymore. Personally, I would love to have an Australian accent. (I used to long for a French accent, but, since meeting Ben, I've switched to longing for an Australian accent.)

In a few minutes the bell rang. I bounded down the stairs and pulled open the front door. "Hi," I greeted Ben. "Come on in."

Ben stepped into the living room and looked around. "Kind of quiet in here, isn't it?" he observed.

"Mom kicked everyone outside for awhile," I explained.

"Oh," said Ben. "The house is a little spooky when it's so quiet."

"Don't worry," I said, leading him into the dining room. "It won't last too long. But hopefully it will last long enough for us to get some work done."

*That* sure turned out to be wishful thinking!

No sooner had we opened our math books on the dining room table than I heard the back door slam. "Let's each do this first problem and see if we come up with the same answer," I suggested to Ben, pointing to a problem in the book.

We were working on the problem when suddenly I jumped up from the table and screamed. Something warm and furry had run across my foot.

Ben jumped up, too. "Mal! What's wrong?"

Then I saw Frodo, our pet hamster, scurrying along the floor by the wall. The sound of laughter came from just outside the dining room.

I stormed to the doorway. There were Adam, Jordan, Byron, and Nicky, red-faced from giggling. "Ha! Ha! Ha!" I said angrily. "You guys are a riot. Someone come get Frodo."

"We haven't seen Frodo," replied Jordan.

Glaring at my brothers, I went back into the room and tried to grab Frodo. Boy, is he fast! It took almost five minutes for Ben and me to catch him.

Once I'd put Frodo in his cage, I returned to the dining room. "Sorry about that," I apologized to Ben.

"It's okay. I finished the first problem while

you were gone. I'll just wait for you to do it."

At that moment, Margo appeared in the doorway. "Excuse me," she said. "Mom wants to know if you and Ben would like some lemonade."

"Sure," I told her. "Thanks."

In minutes Margo came back with the drinks. With her was Claire who carried a tray of still-warm butter cookies Mom had made. "Thanks a lot," said Ben, taking a cookie.

"You're welcome," Claire replied. My sisters can be so sweet sometimes.

"See?" I said to him. "Not all members of my family are geeks."

But the geek patrol was soon back.

The next thing that happened may possibly be the most embarrassing thing that has ever happened to me.

I was working on the first problem when I began to notice this strange sound coming from outside the dining room. It was a slurpy, squeaky sound. It was a kissing sound! And it was loud, amplified. I put down my pen and felt a hot blush burn across my cheeks. (Which only made matters worse.)

"I love you so much," came a silly, deep voice.

"No, I love you more!" This was a high-pitched voice.

"I love *you* more, my darling Mallory!" The deep voice.

"I love you more-est, Benjamin my sweet!" the high squeaky voice squealed. Then there were more loud, wet kissing noises.

I wanted to die! To disappear then and there!

Ben looked like he felt the same way. He was smiling, but he was also blushing.

"Excuse me a minute," I said, pushing back my chair.

When I reached the doorway, I found my darling brothers crowded around Nicky's new speaker phone, busily kissing the backs of their own hands. They looked at me with guilty, but laughing eyes. "I'm going to brain you idiots!" I shouted.

Nicky switched the speaker to baby-talk. "Time to go bye-bye," he said. As he spoke, he raced away behind the triplets, disappearing into the kitchen.

"We're not going to get anything done with them hanging around," I said apologetically, turning back to Ben.

"Want to work at my house?" Ben suggested.

"Good idea," I said as I closed my math notebook. Ben is so nice. Another boy probably would have run out of the house. Why couldn't my brothers be more like him?

I had to let my mother know I was leaving, so I stuck my head into the kitchen. Only Vanessa was there, thumbing through a mail-order toy catalog. "Where's Mom?" I asked.

"In the yard with Claire."

"Tell her I'm going over to Ben's to work," I said. "I have to get away from the Pike punks before I kill them."

"I heard what they were doing," she said sympathetically. "I don't blame you for wanting to murder them."

"Tell me about it," I said, leaving the kitchen.

It didn't take long to walk to Ben's house. The Hobarts moved into Mary Anne's old house across from Claudia's. (Mary Anne Spier and Claudia Kishi are both BSC members and my friends. More about them later.) And, anyway, it was better to work at Ben's house than at mine since I had a BSC meeting that day at five-thirty. The BSC meetings are held at Claudia's so all I would have to do is run across the street.

At Ben's house we were able to sit at the kitchen table and work without being disturbed. His three brothers — James (eight), Mathew (six), and Johnny (four) — are nothing like my brothers. They're actually sweet and well-behaved. They were playing video games in the family den. They didn't bother us even once the entire time.

At about 5:15, I shut my history book. (We finished the math pretty quickly once we escaped from my brothers.) "Gee, it's so peaceful here," I said with a sigh.

"Not always," Ben replied. "Besides, I think your house is fun."

"Try living there," I groaned as I stuffed my books into my pack.

Ben stood up and opened the refrigerator. "Hey, it's a miracle! There's chocolate cake left from last night. Want some?"

I glanced at the kitchen clock. 5:17. "Okay. But I have to eat and run. Kristy starts meetings at five-thirty sharp." Kristy Thomas is the president of the BSC. Punctuality is very important to her.

Ben cut me a slice of cake. "That's okay," he said with a smile. "We have to eat fast, anyway, before my Mom comes in and tells me no cake before supper."

Mrs. Hobart makes a super delicious chocolate cake. She makes it from scratch, too. Until I met Ben, I thought making a cake from scratch meant you started by opening a box of cake mix!

As I sat eating the cake, I thought how great it must be to live at Ben's house. Homemade cake. Quiet, unobnoxious brothers. Heaven!

12

# CHAPTER 2

Although I was only across the street, I was almost late for the BSC meeting. (I was having such a nice time with Ben that I stayed until the absolute last second.) I flew into Claudia's bedroom just as her digital clock turned to 5:30.

Still breathless, I sat down quickly on the floor next to my best friend Jessi Ramsey. "Where were you?" Jessi whispered.

"At Ben's," I whispered back.

Dawn Schafer, who was sitting on the bed behind me, heard what I said. "Ben's!" she teased in a singsong voice.

I could feel myself turn red. "We were doing homework!"

"Ooooohh! At Ben's!" the other club members sang out, laughing. All except Mary Anne. She was there with her boyfriend, Logan Bruno. (He's also a member of the club. I'll tell you how he fits in after I tell you about

13

the club.) It was unusual for Logan to come to meetings. I guess he was at the meeting that day because he had been hanging out with Mary Anne.

"What's wrong with doing homework together?" Mary Anne asked, taking Logan's hand. "Logan and I just came from studying in the library."

"Oooooooooooohhhh!" the club members teased.

Now it was Logan's turn to blush.

"Cut it out, you guys," said Mary Anne.

"Oh, we're just teasing," laughed Stacey McGill, perched cross-legged on Claudia's bed.

"Okay, enough," Kristy said, speaking over the giggles. She looked very stern as she sat forward in Claudia's director's chair with one leg crossed high over the other knee, her pencil stuck over one ear and the club notebook on her lap. "This meeting of the Baby-sitters Club is about to begin!"

Before I go any further, I suppose I should tell you about the club and its members. I'll start with the members and then I'll explain how the club works.

First I'll tell you about Jessi, since she's my best friend. Like me, she's eleven. We're both in the sixth grade at Stoneybrook Middle School. Jessi is tall and beautiful. And African-

American. This was a problem for some people when the Ramseys first came to Stoneybrook. But the Ramsey family stuck it out, and now nobody bothers them about the color of their skin anymore.

Jessi is a ballet dancer. She's already *en pointe*, which means she dances in toe shoes. This proves how gifted she is. She's already danced in several professional productions and has been accepted to this great (and really demanding) ballet school in Stamford (which is about a half hour from Stoneybrook).

Jessi isn't stuck-up about her dancing. Not at all. Everything about her is very normal. She has a normal-sized family: a father, a mother, a sister (Becca, who is eight), and a baby brother named John Philip Jr., also known as Squirt. Her Aunt Cecelia lives with them. She stays home and takes care of things while Mr. and Mrs. Ramsey work.

Despite our differences (one of them being that I can't dance to save my life!), Jessi and I have tons in common. We love to read, especially about horses. Marguerite Henry's horse stories are our favorites. We love to baby-sit. And we are *soooooo* glad to be junior officers in the BSC.

As I've mentioned, the president of the BSC is Kristy Thomas. She has brown hair, brown eyes, and is very short. In fact, I think she's the shortest girl in the eighth grade. When you're around Kristy, though, you don't think of her as a small person. That's because she has such a big personality.

Kristy is loaded with energy. I guess you could call her a tomboy. She almost always wears jeans, a turtleneck shirt, a sweater, and running shoes. She coaches a softball team for little kids called Kristy's Krushers, and she's good at lots of sports.

To be honest, you could say that Kristy has kind of a big mouth and is on the bossy side, but that doesn't bother me. One reason the BSC works so well is that Kristy isn't afraid to take charge.

Besides, I understand how it feels to be part of a big family. (Kristy's family is now as large as mine.) In a big family you have to speak up if you want to be heard. And when you have younger brothers and sisters, you get used to being in charge. Giving orders starts to come naturally.

So, I can appreciate these things about Kristy, even though size is the only thing our families have in common. Unlike my plain old family, Kristy's is a modern blended kind of family. And the story of her family is pretty interesting.

The Thomases started out with two parents and four kids — Kristy, plus two older brothers, Sam and Charlie, and one younger brother, David Michael. When David Michael was still a baby, Mr. Thomas walked out on the family, leaving Mrs. Thomas to raise four kids. (Can you imagine?) For a long time she struggled, but — like Kristy — she's a real dynamo, and she did very well.

After several years, Mrs. Thomas met and fell in love with Watson Brewer, who is (are you ready?) a millionare! He even lives in a mansion.

They got married, and Kristy and her brothers moved into his house. (Believe it or not, Kristy wasn't thrilled about this because she didn't want to move and she didn't like Watson. But now she's used to her new neighborhood and she's changed her mind about her stepfather.) When her mother got married, Kristy's family grew right away. Watson has two kids from his first marriage, Karen and Andrew, who are seven and four. Even though they only stay at Kristy's every other weekend, Kristy has grown close to them. Then, Watson and Kristy's mother adopted Emily Michelle, a little girl from Vietnam, who is two and a half. Finally, Nannie, Kristy's grandmother, moved in to help out with Emily Michelle. That means when Karen and Andrew are over, ten people live in Kristy's house, just like in mine — only I'm sure being spread out in a mansion cuts down on the "pandemonium" quite a bit.

Do I sound jealous? Maybe I am, just a little. But it's nothing against Kristy. She's not snooty. In fact, she's a regular person, and a lot of fun.

Claudia Kishi is the vice-president of the BSC. She has that title mostly because we use her room and her telephone. Like Kristy, Claudia's a lot of fun, but I don't know if you'd call her a "regular person." For starters, Claudia is so beautiful it's almost unbelievable. She's Japanese-American and has this long, silky black hair, and dark, almond-shaped eyes.

But that isn't what makes her different. It's Claudia, herself, who's unique. (Okay, we're all unique.) Everything about Claudia is artistic. She paints, draws, makes pottery. Claudia looks artistic, too. She makes her own jewelry, and she wears her hair and clothing in really trendy, unusual ways.

Today was a good example. Claudia was wearing a pair of soft, balloony, purple pants; a neon green long-sleeve leotard top; a wide, red braided belt; and a pair of soft, red ballet shoes. Her hair was swept into a French braid with wispy tendrils hanging loose. From one ear dangled a long earring made up of small papier-mâché tropical fruit. In the other ear,

18

where she had two holes, Claudia wore two small papier-mâché hoops. (This earring set is her own creation.) If I wore an outfit like that, I'd look like a lunatic. But not Claudia. She looked like a fashion model.

Claudia adores junk food and Nancy Drew books (which she hides around her room because her parents don't approve of either). Here's what she hates: school. She is the worst student. I can't believe the words she spells wrong! Honestly, half the time I think she must be kidding. But she swears she's not. Claudia's teachers say Claudia just doesn't try hard enough. That might be because she doesn't want to be compared to her sixteen-year-old sister, Janine, who is an actual genius. But, anyway, I've never met anyone like Claudia, and I don't think I ever will.

Mary Anne Spier is our club secretary. She looks a bit like Kristy (who is one of her two best friends). They're both short with brown hair and eyes. But Mary Anne is very different from Kristy. She's quiet and sensitive. She cries easily. And while Kristy is a talker, Mary Anne is a listener. She's a very sweet person.

Mary Anne's mother died when she was small. For a long time, the Spier family was just Mary Anne and her father. Mr. Spier was very over-protective. Even in the seventh grade, Mary Anne still wore braids and these dumpy little-kid jumpers. But now she looks much more fashionable. That's because Mr. Spier has loosened up a lot.

At this point, I have to stop and tell you about Dawn. Dawn is not only Mary Anne's other best friend, she's her stepsister!

Dawn is our alternate officer. That means she has to be ready to fill in for any other member who can't come to a BSC meeting for some reason. Dawn has long, long, long white-blonde hair and a casual-but-trendy way of dressing. (For example, today she was wearing black stirrup pants, a long, fleecy red-and-pink rose-print top and black high-top sneakers. She has two holes pierced in each ear. In those she wore four matching sparkly rose earrings.) Dawn is very pretty, but doesn't seem aware of it. I like that about her.

Another interesting thing about Dawn is that she only eats healthy food. No junk food at all, and she doesn't eat red meat. (I admire that, but I don't think I could do it.) Dawn also likes ghost stories and thinks her house might be haunted. There is even a real secret passageway leading from her bedroom to the old barn behind her house, which is now also Mary Anne's house.

Here's how that happened.

When Dawn first moved to Stoneybrook with her mother and younger brother, Jeff, she didn't know anyone. Her mother was originally from Stoneybrook and had moved back here from California after she and Mr. Schafer got divorced. I think she wanted to be close to her parents (Dawn's grandparents), who still live in Stoneybrook.

The first person to befriend Dawn was Mary Anne. Then an amazing thing happened. While looking through Mrs. Schafer's old high school yearbook one day, Dawn and Mary Anne discovered that long ago their parents had dated in high school. They arranged for their parents to meet again and . . . Mr. Spier and Mrs. Schafer fell in love again. They dated for what seemed like an eternity, but finally they got married. Now they all live together in the Schafers' big farmhouse. (Except for Jeff, who went back to California to live with his dad.) Of course, everyone didn't adjust to this new situation overnight. But now they all seem pretty happy to me.

Last, but not least (as they say) is Stacey McGill. She's our treasurer and a real math whiz. Before moving to Stoneybrook, Stacey lived in New York City. You can tell she's a city girl. She's a lot more sophisticated than the rest of us; even slightly more so than Claudia, who is her best friend. Stacey dresses with great style (though not quite as artistically as Claudia). She has shoulder-length blonde hair, which she usually wears permed, and big, gorgeous blue eyes.

I think Stacey is a little too thin, but that's probably because she has diabetes. A bad form of it, too. She can't eat sweets, except for a little fruit, and she has to give herself injections of insulin every single day. Everyday, forever! I can't *imagine* that! Stacey handles it pretty well, though, and hardly ever complains.

Besides being a diabetic, Stacey has had to deal with a lot of difficult things. First, her father got transferred *back* to New York from Stoneybrook. So just when Stacey was all settled in and happy here, she had to move again. (The Ramsey family moved into the McGills' old house.) Then, when she was back in New York, her parents decided to split up. Her mother decided to come back, *again*, to Stoneybrook. We were all really glad to see Stacey.

Oh, and just so you know, the club also has two associate members, Shannon Kilbourne, and Logan Bruno. Shannon lives across the street from Kristy. And Logan is Mary Anne's boyfriend (remember?) (He speaks with this wonderful drawl, since he's from Kentucky.) They don't *usually* attend meetings, but if none of the regular club members can take a job, we call them.

Now I'm ready to tell you about the club. Kristy got the idea for it one day when she saw her mother making a million phone calls trying to find a baby-sitter for David Michael. It ocurred to Kristy that it would be great if her mother could call one number and get in touch with a whole bunch of baby-sitters at once. That was when she thought up the idea for the Baby-sitters Club.

Immediately, Kristy told Mary Anne and Claudia. They thought the idea was great. Then they decided they needed at least four members, so Claudia suggested Stacey.

The logical place for them to set up headquarters was in Claudia's room since she has her own private phone line. (No one else does. Stacey has an extension, but not her own number.) They wrote an announcement about their club and placed it in the *Stoneybrook News*. Then they made up fliers and passed them out all over the neighborhood. They were in business! They received job calls at their very first meeting.

Soon the club had more business than it could handle. Dawn joined and that helped some. But then Stacey had to leave, and the club was back to four members. That's when they asked Jessi and me to come in as junior officers. We're *junior* because we can only sit in the afternoons, not at night. But that frees the others up for sitting jobs in the evenings. Then Stacey came back, and the BSC had seven members. That's fine, though. We just keep getting more and more work. There're plenty of jobs for everyone.

This is how the club works. We hold meetings every Monday, Wednesday, and Friday between five-thirty and six o'clock. That's when parents call Claudia's number. Someone answers the phone and takes down information about the sitting job. The phone answerer then says she'll call the parent back. Once she hangs up, we put our heads together and see who can take the job.

Mary Anne keeps the club record book. (Another one of Kristy's great ideas.) The record book holds all our important information: clients' names, addresses, and phone numbers; how much each client pays; important notes about the children such as if they're allergic to anything. But most important, it contains everyone's schedule. In it are my orthodontist appointments, Jessi's dance class schedule, Kristy's softball practice schedule, birthdays. You name it, it's in there! This is how we know who is available to sit and when. Mary Anne keeps the book better than a professional secretary. She has never, *ever*, made one scheduling error.

Once Mary Anne checks the book, she tells us who is free to take the job. We decide who will do it, then we call the client back and tell him whom to expect.

Sometimes the phone rings constantly for the entire half hour. Other times, it's a little slower. But no matter what, the half hour whizzes by. There's so much to do.

Stacey keeps track of how much money each of us has been paid. And she collects the dues. No one is crazy about that, but it has to be done. We need the money to help Claudia pay her phone bill, and to pay Charlie Thomas (Kristy's oldest brother) to drive her to meetings, since her new neighborhood is kind of far away.

We also use the money to resupply our Kid-Kits. (*Another* great Kristy idea!) Kid-Kits are boxes filled with crayons, coloring books, our old toys, and lots of fun stuff for the kids to play with. The kits keep the kids busy, and have helped distract kids who were unhappy for one reason or another.

If any money is left over, we use it for something fun, like a slumber party or a pizza lunch. That's the good part about paying dues.

While all this is going on, we're also busy with the club notebook. Members are doing one of two things with it: reading it, or writing in it. The notebook is a diary of our baby-sitting experiences. Some club members hate to write in it, but not me. I also like to read it. It's interesting and very helpful. You can learn how the other baby-sitters solved sitting problems.

We were in the middle of discussing whether or not we should buy these little rubber pop-up suction toys for the Kid-Kits or if they were too dangerous for the youngest kids, when the phone rang.

"Hello, Mrs. Bruno," said Claudia, rolling her eyes playfully at Logan. "Sure. Someone can sit for Hunter and Kerry. But why not just ask Logan?"

Logan began waving his hands and shaking his head.

"I see ... I see ..." Claudia spoke into the phone. "Well, all right. I'll call you back. 'Bye."

"What's up, Logan?" Kristy asked.

"I complained to my mom that I'm tired of baby-sitting all the time. I guess she's trying to take some of the load off me," he explained. "I'll bet she wants you next Tuesday at seven so she and Dad can go to a PTA meeting together."

"Exactly right," Claud confirmed.

Mary Anne opened the record book and

studied it. Then she bit her lip and looked at Logan. "Nobody is free that night. I guess a lot of parents are going to that meeting."

"I really wanted to watch a football game at Pete Black's house that night. He gets the sports channel. Why don't you call Shannon?" said Logan.

Claud dialed Shannon, but she was busy. "Oh, okay," Logan said with a sigh. "I guess I'll have to do it."

Claud called Mrs. Bruno back and gave her the news. Her baby-sitter would be Logan. "Your mother said to tell you she tried her best," said Claudia to Logan as she hung up the phone.

Logan shrugged. "I wish her better luck next time."

Several minutes later the meeting ended. We gathered our things and headed down Claudia's stairs. When I hit the outside air, it sent a shiver up my spine. "Boy, it's getting cold," I said to Jessi. "I hope it's warmer Monday. Otherwise we'll freeze outside during gym."

Jessi turned up her jacket collar as we walked across the yard. "No we won't," she told me. "We're not playing field hockey anymore. Monday we switch to volleyball."

"Yuck! Volleyball," I grumbled.

"I don't mind volleyball so much," said Jessi. "But this year we're going to be playing with the boys."

I stopped dead in my tracks. "The boys! Are you sure?"

"Sure I'm sure. Don't you remember Ms. Walden telling us about it in September?"

Now that she mentioned it, I did. I suppose I'd blocked it from my mind — the way people do when they are presented with facts too horrible to conceive of.

I was expected to appear in front of a bunch of boys in my gross, disgusting gym suit and demonstrate that I was probably the most klutzy, uncoordinated girl in the sixth grade.

# CHAPTER 3

Monday morning my eyes snapped open before the alarm even rang. It was gym day. The day of doom!

Rubbing my eyes, I stumbled out of bed and pulled open my closet door. I fished through the jumble of clothes until, way in the back, I found a one-piece denim jumpsuit. It had been a present for my last birthday. I never wear it. Not because I hate it or anything. It's just not *me*. It's a little too high-style or something.

But it would be perfect for today. With one zip I could step into it and zoom out that door after gym class. No buckles and buttons to slow me down. It was important that I be able to get out of there fast. I had to disappear into the hall and get to my next class as soon as possible. I didn't want any pitying — or worse, laughing — eyes staring at me in the locker room. After all, I had no doubt that this was going to be the most mortifying day of my entire life.

"Did the alarm ring?" Vanessa asked sleepily from under the covers.

"No. I just got up, that's all," I snapped. Vanessa made a face at me. I couldn't blame her. Even I was surprised at how crabby I sounded.

"What's the matter with you?" she grumbled as she swung her legs out of bed.

"Nothing. Sorry," I answered. I didn't even want to talk about it.

At breakfast, Mom kept looking at me strangely. Maybe it was because I was wearing the jumpsuit. Or maybe it was because I was stirring my Cheerios round and round without taking a bite. I had no appetite at all.

"Mal, is something wrong?" she asked at last.

"Nothing except that I look disgusting in my gym suit and I inherited totally unathletic genes from someone," I blurted out.

"Don't look at your mother and me," said my father, coming into the kitchen. "We play a mean game of tennis."

I stood and gathered my books. "Then it was probably some great-aunt who died from embarrassment one day during a volleyball game or whatever they played back then."

"I'm sure you're blowing this out of proportion, Mallory," my mother said sympathetically. "Is there anything we can do to help?"

"No," I replied. Then my eyes lit with an idea. "Maybe I could stay home today. I'd study in my room all day long. I promise."

For one shining moment, I thought I had a chance. My mother looked at my father as if she were considering saying okay.

Then, once again, my *charming* brothers ruined everything.

"Us, too! Us, too!" the triplets cried out.

"No fair!" Nicky protested loudly. "If they're staying home I want to stay home, too."

"Pipe down!" said my father. "Nobody's staying home today. Now, all of you, keep moving."

I went to school, but I probably would have learned more that day if I *had* stayed in my room and studied. I didn't hear a word my teachers said. All I could do was sit and count the minutes until the dreaded gym hour arrived — and plan how to get out of it.

Fantasies raced through my head. I suppose that since I want to be a writer when I'm older (I want to write and illustrate children's books) it's natural for me to make up stories. Let me tell you, I came up with some doozies that morning.

My favorite of all was the one in which I was hit on the head with a volleyball in the first second of the game. I had to be rushed to the hospital where I developed amnesia. Everyone felt extremely guilty that they'd forced me to play. "If only we'd let her stay home," my mother said sorrowfully to my father.

That story gave me an idea. I could (if I had the nerve) pretend to faint dead away on the floor. Preferably this would happen in the locker room so I wouldn't have to appear in public in my gym suit.

It was with this plan in the back of my mind that I headed toward gym class. I realized it was a rather drastic plan, but this was a desperate situation.

"Hi," Jessi greeted me when I entered the locker room.

I wiggled my fingers at her in a half-hearted greeting as I pulled open a locker three doors away from hers. Now I had a decision to make. Should I fill her in on my plan? No. Jessi is a very honest person and she can't lie to save her life. If she knew I was faking, her face would tip everyone off. Besides, she'd probably try to talk me out of it.

"That jumpsuit looks cool on you," she commented as she changed into her baggy blue shorts and white camp-style shirt. Somehow the gym suit doesn't look nearly as bad on her as it does on me. In fact, it looks almost nice. But Jessi looks good in anything.

"Oh, this? Thanks," I muttered. My mind was on my plan. I had to find just the right moment to drop to the floor.

But the right moment never seemed to come. The truth was that I couldn't get up the nerve to do it. And time was running out. Soon almost all the girls were dressed and moving out to the gym.

"Are you coming, Mal?" Jessi asked.

"Um, yeah. You go ahead," I told her. That was the problem. I couldn't do it in front of Jessi. I'd feel too dumb.

"Okay, you better hurry," said Jessi, heading for the door.

This is it, I told myself. Now! I squinched my eyes shut and crumpled to the floor.

I waited, expecting to hear a wave of shocked and concerned voices begin to gather around me.

I didn't hear anything.

What was going on? Hadn't anyone noticed? Didn't anyone care that I was lying in a pathetic heap on the floor?

Cautiously, I squinked open one eye. No one was around. I lifted my head and looked.

That's when I realized the humiliating truth. I'd waited too long. No one was left in the locker room.

With a deep sigh, I pulled myself up onto the bench. At that moment, my gym teacher, Ms. Walden, came barrelling back into the locker room from the gym outside. "Pike," she barked when she saw me, "you're late! Get dressed and get out there."

She pulled open a supply cabinet and rummaged inside.

I got dressed, not knowing what else to do.

In a minute, Ms. Walden emerged from the closet with two big cardboard boxes. "Ms. Walden, I don't feel so — " I began in a small voice.

She didn't hear me. Instead she plunked one of the boxes on the bench by me. "Here, you can carry one of these out for me. And get a move on!"

With that she was gone. I peeked into the box. It was filled with blue, red, orange, and green colored cotton pinnies. The only thing that could make our gym suits look uglier than they already were was to put a crumpled, faded pinny over it. It was the finishing touch.

But now I had no choice but to go out to the gym. They were waiting for me to bring the rest of the pinnies. There was nothing to do but go.

I dressed and went out to the gym. Normally the gym is divided into two parts by a movable wall. The boys take gym on one side and the girls on the other. Today the wall was moved aside the way it is for basketball games.

On the bleachers at the far side of the gym sat the sixth-grade boys, a combined class of about forty boys listening to their gym teacher, Mr. De Young.

Four volleyball nets had been set up on each side of the gym. There was no getting away from it. This was really happening. The only good thing about the situation was that Ben didn't have gym this period. That would have meant one perfectly great boyfriend down the drain, for sure.

My classmates were seated on the bleachers closest to me. In front of them stood Ms. Walden showing them something on a rolling blackboard. She motioned for me to bring the box to her. I set it down beside her and found a spot on the bleacher. "Pike, write your name on a piece of paper and drop it in that basket," Ms. Walden said, pointing to a basket on the bottom bleacher. "We're picking teams at random. You'll play with these same teammates for the entire volleyball unit."

This was good news and bad news. The bad news was that I might not be on the same team as Jessi. And I had been counting on having her near to make jokes and wisecracks through this ordeal. The good news was that I wouldn't have to be crushed by the fact that no one would pick me for their team. This way, my teammates would have no choice. They'd be stuck with me, like it or not.

As Ms. Walden continued to review the rules of volleyball with the help of her blackboard drawings, I dropped my name in the basket. When she was done, Ms. Walden joined Mr. De Young in the center of the gym and they combined the names. Then came the long, drawn-out process of pulling out the names and separating everyone into different teams. I prayed it would take up the entire period.

Jessi scooted over beside me on the bleacher. "You look terrible. Do you feel all right?" she asked.

"I'm going to make a total jerk of myself," I told her. "And in front of all these boys!"

"Everyone will be paying attention to their own game," she pointed out.

"Yeah, and the kids on my team will be paying attention to me, because I'll be the worst player on the team."

Jessi gave my arm a friendly squeeze. "You're not that bad."

I looked at her. How could she be so calm? And why did her gym suit look so good on her? "Do you iron your gym suit?" I asked.

"Aunt Cecelia does. She irons everything. Even underwear," Jessi replied with a laugh.

My outfit had the casual, rumpled look that can only be achieved by taking my shorts and shirt straight from the dryer and stuffing them into my knapsack. I made a mental note to iron my gym suit.

"Mallory Pike, green team," Ms. Walden called out.

"So long," I told Jessi as I slid off the bleacher.

"It won't be as bad as you think," she said, smiling. Good old Jessi. She had no idea.

The green team was to play at the net at the far end of the gym. I felt as if I were walking in slow motion, and everyone in the gym was staring at me. I had never been so aware of my arms before. Suddenly I had no idea what to do with them. I crossed them, but that felt dumb. Then I put them behind my back, but that made me look like I was in handcuffs. I placed them at my sides and felt like a robot.

"Move, Pike," called Ms. Walden, clapping her hands.

Thank you, Ms. Walden, I said to myself. Now everyone really is looking at me. I broke into a trot and that, at least, made me forget about my arms.

When I reached the net, a girl named Helen

Gallway handed me a green pinny. Helen is one of those very athletic girls Ms. Walden just adores. Somehow it seemed to be understood that she was the team captain.

"Mallory, how's your serve?" Helen asked me.

"Not so hot," I admitted.

Helen sighed. "Okay then, stand in the middle over to the right."

I did as she said, hoping I was in a nice, out-of-the-way spot that the ball would never reach. I looked around at my ten teammates, but didn't see anyone I knew very well. In a minute, Mr. De Young blew his whistle and the games began.

The other team chose a big guy named Chris Brooks to deliver their first serve. Obviously Chris was a good judge of nonathletes. He served the ball directly to me.

"Yaow!" I cried, jumping back. The ball came at me so fast it practically whomped my head off! (My fantasy of being rushed to the hospital had nearly come true.)

"Ma-lor-reeeee!" Helen said huffily. "You're supposed to hit the ball, not run away from it."

"Sorry," I said lamely.

But, too bad for me, Chris Brooks had realized he was onto a winning strategy. Here was his plan: Keep sending the ball to Mallory. Which is exactly what he did.

"Put your arms up," a boy named Glen Johnson coached from behind me. I tried that, but the next ball just flew right through them.

"It helps if you keep your eyes open, too," Glen added snidely as he tossed the ball back over the net to the other team.

"Right, yeah. I know that. Sorry," I mumbled.

After two more misses, I could tell my team was pretty annoyed with me. Hey! Don't look at me! I felt like shouting. I didn't ask to play this stupid game!

"No matter what happens, let me get it," said a boy named Robbie Mara, who was standing next to me.

"Gladly," I replied sarcastically. I should have been relieved, but his superior tone of voice bugged me.

Once again, the ball came zooming at my head, like a missile aimed at its target. "Move, move, move," I heard Robbie say. But I didn't move fast enough.

The next thing I knew he was leaping in front of me, hurling himself at the ball. His arm jabbed me in the side. His foot came down hard on mine. Suddenly I lost my balance and went flying over backward. I landed with a thud on my behind on the gym floor.

And was anyone concerned about me? Oh, no! Everyone was cheering because we had finally made a point.

"Pike, are you okay?" asked Ms. Walden, who was moving from game to game.

I didn't know which was worse, the pain in my foot, or the embarrassment. Hot tears tingled in my eyes, but I didn't want anyone to see them. "I'm all right," I mumbled, staggering to my feet.

"Get in there after that ball," she told me. "You're wimping out on your team."

Thanks for making that so clear, I thought bitterly. Just in case anyone here wasn't aware of that.

Once my team had the ball the game wasn't so bad. At least every serve wasn't directed at me. And I discovered that if I hopped up and down with my arms in the air, I could pretend to be a functioning member of the team.

I didn't fool Ms. Walden, though. "Pike! Don't just flap your arms!" she'd yell. "This is your ball, Pike! Get it!"

So, thanks to Ms. Walden's big mouth, all eyes were on me every time the ball flew past me.

The game seemed endless. I couldn't help but wonder what terrible thing I'd done to deserve this torture. Ms. Walden never let up on me.

The girls on my team weren't too bad. (With the exception of Helen.) But the boys were animals. You'd think they were engaged in a war, the way they yelled, leaped, pounded the ball, and spiked it over the net. Didn't they realize it was just a game?

After what seemed like a thousand years, the period ended. As I slunk off the court, I realized Jessi had been right. It hadn't been as bad as I thought.

It had been much worse.

# CHAPTER 4

$A$fter school, I dropped my books at home, then limped to my afternoon baby-sitting job on Bradford Court.

My foot still throbbed from when that jerk Robbie had stomped on it. And to say that I was in a bad mood would be an understatement. But I could feel my mood lift a little as I approached the Newtons' house. I like sitting for them. Four-year-old Jamie is lots of fun and Lucy is one of the most adorable babies in the world. She has the biggest, roundest blue eyes you have ever seen.

"Hi, Mallory," Mrs. Newton said as she opened the door and let me in. "Did you hurt your foot?"

"Some guy stepped on it during gym."

"Ouch," Mrs. Newton sympathized. "Well, I hope the kids don't give you too much trouble. I'm afraid Jamie has been acting up today."

I smiled confidently at Mrs. Newton. "Jamie's never any problem. And Lucy's an angel."

That seemed to make Mrs. Newton relax. To tell the truth, she *did* look frazzled, which usually isn't the case. "We'll be fine," I added.

Mrs. Newton gave me the phone number of the hairdresser's where she'd be for the next two hours. "I'll try to get home earlier, if I can," she said. "I know you have your meeting at five-thirty."

"Thanks," I said. "If you get here by five-fifteen, I'll have just enough time to race over there."

"Lucy is down for her nap and Jamie is upstairs in his room coloring," she continued as she pulled on her coat. "I finally got him settled down. He's been wild lately. I don't know if it's nursery school, or if he's competing with Lucy for attention or what."

"Don't worry. Enjoy your haircut," I said.

"Highlighting."

"Whatever."

When she was gone, I quietly headed up the stairs. When I reached the second floor, I saw about a hundred crayons spread across the floor in the hallway. Jamie was busy peeling the paper off of them and then cracking each one in half.

"Jamie! What are you doing?" I cried softly,

aware of the sleeping baby across the hall.

Jamie grinned at me guiltily. "Making rockets."

"What?"

To demonstrate, Jamie picked up one of the broken crayons. "Fire rocket!" he shouted as he hurled the crayon against Lucy's closed door.

"Don't do that," I told him, picking my way through the crayons. "You're going to wake Lucy and you're marking up her door. Besides that, you're going to ruin all your crayons."

"I don't care," he replied.

"Sure you do," I said as I began to gather up the crayons.

Suddenly, Jamie scooped up a handful of crayons and sprang to his feet. "No, I *don't* care!" he insisted. With that, he hurled an entire handful of crayons at Lucy's door.

My jaw dropped. I had never seen Jamie act this way. "Jamie! What's the matter?"

"I want to call up my friend, Roger," said Jamie stubbornly. "He's my best friend in school. He's five!"

"First we're picking up all these crayons," I said firmly.

"I want to call Roger!" Jamie bellowed.

At that moment, a piercing cry told me he'd awakened Lucy. "Now look what you've done," I scolded, pushing open Lucy's door.

In the darkened nursery, Lucy sat up in her crib wearing a yellow one-piece stretchy. Her big eyes were sleepy and wet with tears. And when she saw me, she began to wail even harder. Babies prefer to see their mothers when they wake from a nap. But I lifted her out of her crib and walked around with her. In about three minutes she had calmed down. After another three minutes, she gave me a big smile.

"Hey, Jamie!" I cried. "She has four teeth. She only had two the last time I was here."

"Big deal," said Jamie, who had come into the room with me.

I studied him a minute and decided Mrs. Newton had been right. He did seem to resent Lucy. And maybe Roger had something to do with his attitude, too. I've noticed that when Nicky wants the triplets to hang around with him, he acts tough so they won't think he's a baby. Possibly Jamie was trying to act like Roger.

As I supported Lucy on my shoulder, with one hand under her bottom, I realized that her diaper was leaking at the sides. "Time for a fresh diaper, kiddo," I said, laying her on her changing table.

At least Lucy's temperament was the same. She kicked and laughed as I changed her diaper. "She's gotten so big," I commented to

45

Jamie while I fished in Lucy's drawer for a fresh romper. "You'll see. The older she gets, the more fun she'll be to play with. Right now she probably seems like a pain to you sometimes."

There was no answer. I looked around and saw that Jamie had left the room. Considering the mood he was in, I didn't want to let him out of my sight for too long. I quickly snapped Lucy into her outfit and took her from the table. "Let's go find your grouchy big brother," I whispered to her as we left her nursery.

The first place I checked was Jamie's room. He wasn't there. Then I tried the den and the kitchen. "Jamie!" I called out. "Jamie!"

With Lucy still in my arms, I checked the basement. "Jamie!" I looked behind the washer and dryer, around the boiler. Everywhere.

Finally I returned to the living room. "Jamie! This isn't funny!" I hollered. Still no response.

Now I was starting to panic. I went to the front door and looked out. He wasn't in the front yard. Next I tried the backyard. No Jamie.

Lucy must have sensed my growing unhappiness because she began to whimper. "It's okay," I consoled her.

My arms were getting tired from carrying her, so I put her in her high chair in the kitchen. Luckily she became interested in some plastic toys that were on the tray, which freed me to look around for Roger's phone number or address. All I could think of was that Jamie had gone to his house.

I did find the number of a Roger Friedman tacked to the bulletin board. I called it, but the line was busy. "Get off the phone," I mumbled as I banged down the receiver. If the line didn't clear in the next few minutes, I planned to call the operator for an emergency break-in.

"Stay calm, Mallory," I told myself. "He's got to be here somewhere."

But all the horrible possibilities occurred to me. What if he'd headed for Roger's house and gotten lost? Or hit by a car? Or kidnapped?

I decided to dress Lucy more warmly and go outside to look for him. I picked her up from the seat and carried her back upstairs. Then I dressed her in her warm, fleecy sack suit, put on her hat, and carried her downstairs again.

Before we left, I decided to try the Roger Friedman number one more time. I wasn't even sure this was the right Roger, but it was worth a try. With Lucy propped against my

47

hip, the phone receiver cradled between my shoulder and cheek, I punched in the number. The line was still busy.

"All right, Lucy, let's go," I said.

At that moment I smelled the distinctive aroma of a dirty diaper. "What next?" I sighed. Normally, I don't mind changing a dirty diaper, but this diaper change presented a real dilemma. Should I waste precious time unbundling her, or, should I take her as she was and risk her getting a rash?

It was a decision I didn't have to make.

"Boo!" shouted Jamie, sneaking up behind me.

I nearly jumped to the ceiling. I hadn't heard him approaching at all. "Ohmigosh!" I breathed, clutching Lucy.

Jamie doubled over with laughter. "Got ya! Got ya good!"

"You scared me to death!" I cried angrily. "I didn't know where you were!"

"I know. I was hiding," Jamie told me proudly.

"That's not a funny trick," I told him. "Don't do it again."

"It is *so* funny," Jamie said, pouting. "You're just an old grouch-head!"

"Well, you're a hider-head," I replied. This may have been a very immature response, and it made no sense, but there was no reason to stay mad at him.

"Then you're a spider-head," he replied.

"You're a fighter-head," I shot back. That was a bad choice.

"No, I'm a fighter pilot!" Jamie shouted. He spread his arms and, with loud engine noises, began to zoom around the house.

Lucy laughed at the noise as I unbundled her. But in seconds, a loud crash came from the living room.

"Uh-oh," I heard Jamie say.

With Lucy in my arms, I ran into the room and found a glass vase smashed across the floor. Tiny slivers of glass glistened everywhere. "The wing of my jet accidentally knocked it over," Jamie said sheepishly.

"I hope it wasn't an expensive vase," I replied.

Jamie shrugged. The way my luck was running today, it was probably priceless.

"Hey, pew, she stinks," Jamie observed, pointing to Lucy.

"I know," I replied. "Let's go upstairs and change her. Then we'll come down and clean up this glass."

"No way! I'm not getting near that diaper," said Jamie, backing away. He spotted a jagged piece of glass on the floor and bent over it.

"Hey, this one looks like a little glass — "

"Don't touch that," I said. He didn't listen.

"Ouch! Ouch! Ouuwwww!" he howled, clutching his hand. A ribbon of blood flowed from his thumb.

I rushed him into the kitchen and put Lucy back in her high chair. I could see that the cut wasn't *that* deep, it was just bleeding a lot. I put pressure on his thumb to help stop the bleeding and pretty soon it was only a trickle. There was no need to call a doctor or the hospital. All I had to do was clean the cut and put on a bandage.

Unfortunately, Jamie wasn't nearly as calm as I was. He screeched hysterically and struggled with me as I tried to hold his hand under cold running water at the sink. With all the commotion, Lucy started screaming.

Glancing at the kitchen clock, I saw that I had only been at the Newtons' for a half hour! It felt like years.

In fact, this was turning out to be one of the longest — and worst — days I could remember.

# CHAPTER 5

Sunday

You would think that baby-sitting for your own brother and sister would be the easiest job on earth. Wrong! At least it wasn't easy the other day. Becca was great, but Squirt was a monster. Aunt Cecelia says "the terrible twos" start before a baby is actually two years old. That must be true. Because Squirt isn't two yet, but my experience baby-sitting for him sure was terrible!

Usually Jessi doesn't have to sit for Becca and Squirt. Aunt Cecelia is almost always there to look after them. But last Sunday Aunt Cecelia needed to go to the hospital to visit a friend of hers who was a patient. Mr. and Mrs. Ramsey had volunteered to work at a PTA-sponsored craft show. So Jessi was baby-sitting.

That was fine with her. Becca and Squirt are never any trouble. But that's what I said about Jamie Newton. And look what had happened! This turned out to be a similar situation.

Now that Squirt can walk, he's into every-thing. As soon as Aunt Cecelia left, he pulled a lace runner off a side table, sending every-thing crashing to the floor. Jessi no sooner picked up the stuff (luckily nothing broke) than he pulled open the drawer where the Ramseys keep their phone books and began tearing pages from them.

Jessi is a patient person, but Squirt never let up. She even made him his latest favorite food, macaroni and cheese. When she presented it to him, he flung it away, spraying the kitchen with sticky, orange macaroni.

Speaking of spraying the kitchen, Becca wound up making quite a mess even though she was *trying* to be good. She was studying nutrition in school, and her weekend homework assignment was to make a healthy drink in the blender and bring a thermos of it into class on Monday. The kids were going to sample each drink and vote on which was the best.

"I think the noise of the blender is making Squirt even crankier," Becca said to Jessi as she fed a carrot into the machine.

"Everything is making him cranky," replied Jessi, who was helping Becca with the project. She'd borrowed a health-food cookbook from Dawn. Dawn had even pointed out one of her favorite drinks. Now Jessi was reading the instructions as Becca pureéd the ingredients in the blender.

At the moment, Jessi was allowing Squirt to play on the floor with the pots and pans he'd pulled from the kitchen cabinets. It would be a pain to put them back later, but Jessi was willing to do that if they would keep Squirt happy for awhile — at least until she and Becca could finish making the health drink.

"Do you have the can of beet juice opened?" Jessi asked. Becca nodded. "It says to pour that in while blending on a low speed," Jessi read.

"While the blender is running?" Becca questioned.

Jessi checked the book and nodded. "That's what it says."

"Okay, here goes," said Becca. She found

the lowest speed on the blender, turned it on, and slowly began to pour.

Jessi glanced at Squirt. His lower lip was trembling. The slow drone of the blender did seem to be annoying him. He picked up two wooden spoons and banged on the pots, as if to drown out the noise.

Finally Becca turned off the blender. "Whoaw! It's almost over the top," she commented. Gingerly, she lifted the blender off the stand.

Bang! Clang! Squirt had climbed to his feet and was now throwing the pots and pans across the kitchen floor. "That's enough, Squirt," said Jessi. She tried to take a pot lid from his hand. "Give me that and we'll go look at some books," she added. But Squirt was not going to give her the lid.

"No!" he cried. (That's one of Squirt's few words.)

"This doesn't taste bad at all," Becca said as she sipped some of her drink from a teaspoon.

"Dawn said it was good," commented Jessi. Then she turned back to Squirt. "No more throwing pans, okay, Squirt?" she said.

"No!" Squirt shouted again. And this time, he hurled the pot lid just as Becca was turning to carry the full blender to the refrigerator.

Bang! The lid hit Becca.

"Oh, no!" she cried as the blender fell from

her hands, splashing purple juice everywhere.

Jessi closed her eyes briefly.

"Sorry," whispered Becca.

"It's not your fault," Jessi told her. "But look at this place!"

"Look at my new sweater," added Becca.

Jessi sighed, noticing that Squirt was tracking purple footprints across the kitchen floor and was about to go into the living room. "Stop, Squirt!" she cried, grabbing him.

"This is impossible," she added. Jessi thought quickly. She couldn't let Aunt Cecelia come home to this mess. "I know," she told Becca. "How about inviting Charlotte Johanssen over. The two of you can watch Squirt while I clean up."

"Sure," said Becca. Charlotte is her best friend, so she was happy to ask her over.

Ten minutes later, Charlotte arrived. "Don't let him out of your sight," Jessi instructed the girls as she sent Squirt off with them. Then she set to cleaning the kitchen. This took awhile. Beet juice was everywhere! She had to do a whole load of purple-stained laundry. The tablecloth, the kitchen curtains, dishcloths, and Becca's sweater all had to be put in the washer. The drink had sprayed all over the pots and pans, so every one of them had to be washed as well. Not to mention, the floor, the cabinets, and the legs of the kitchen chairs. Furthermore, the blender had cracked up the side. What was left of the drink ran down Jessi's arm when she picked it up. Yechh.

By the time Aunt Cecelia returned, the kitchen was clean. And Jessi was extremely happy to see her aunt. Becca and Charlotte had managed to keep Squirt out of trouble. They'd accomplished this by allowing him to throw his blocks all over the rec room. Poor Jessi. She felt obligated to pick them up, too. After all, she'd been left in charge.

"I was *exhaust*ed," Jessi told me. "I don't know what was wrong with Squirt."

I didn't say anything to her then, but I was beginning to develop a theory about Squirt. Also about Jamie Newton, Robbie Mara, and my brothers. What did they all have in common? That they were big pains? Yes. And also that they were boys.

# CHAPTER 6

It's amazing how fast time flies when you don't want gym class to come again. But, in a flash, it arrived. Before I knew it, it was Wednesday. Time for *Gym Class 2. The horror continues.*

And boy was it horrible!

The night before, my mother nearly fainted when she saw me ironing my gym shorts. I thought it would make a big difference. The only difference it made was that in class the next day, I no longer looked like a rumpled gangly scarecrow with bony knees and elbows. Instead, I looked like a neat scarecrow with bony knees and elbows. Not a huge improvement.

So, there I was once again, standing out on this gigantic court with kids I barely knew, ready to be mocked, humiliated, shouted at, and possibly stepped on. I'm sure you can understand this put me in a pretty bad mood.

Bad is not the word. Foul, livid, murderous: those are probably more accurate words.

And my theory about boys being major pains — much more so than girls — was beginning to seem very true. I now saw that it was a wise person who orginally decided to separate boys and girls during gym classes. Boys are crazed when it comes to sports. Take that day, for example. They were throwing the ball around, grunting and shouting. And the game hadn't even started yet. They reminded me of a bunch of toddlers who had somehow gotten their hands on too much sugar.

Once the game *did* start, they were out of control. They didn't care who they knocked over, or elbowed out of the way. They hit that ball as if they were trying to hurt somebody.

During the first game, came the moment feared by everyone on my team — especially me. It was my turn to serve. Just in case I wasn't already nervous enough, Ms. Walden wandered over to terrorize me with her less-than-helpful advice.

As I was about to serve the ball, she shouted: "A fist, Pike! Hit it with your fist. Not open-handed!"

She rattled me so that I let the ball roll out of my hand and had to go chasing it through the gym. Talk about your embarrassing moments!

Everyone looked impatient when I returned. So, just to get rid of the stupid thing, I served the ball quickly.

I served it into the net.

"Don't *tap* the ball, Pike! Hit it hard!" (In case you couldn't guess, that was the ever-helpful Ms. Walden.)

My next serve went *under* the net.

"Straight arm, Pike! Your arm is wobbling all over the place," Ms. Walden shouted.

You can't imagine how much I wished Ms. Walden would go away. If I could have, I would have paid her all my baby-sitting money to shut up and leave.

"Pike, this is your last serve. You better make it count."

It counted, all right. For the other team. I shot the ball up in the air, and watched it bounce right back down at my feet.

"When Gallway serves, watch her," Ms. Walden advised me.

"Okay," I muttered as I rotated out of the serving position and up to the front line, making room for Helen Gallway to serve the next time my team got the ball.

"You watch her closely," Ms. Walden added as she moved on to harass someone else on another team. "Gallway has a mean serve."

Well, I was very happy for Helen Gallway, but having a mean serve was not exactly my ambition in life. What did Ms. Walden think? That they were going to put that on my grave? Here lies Mallory Pike. She had a *mean serve!* Not! It didn't matter to me, so I didn't see why everyone had to make such a big deal over it. I couldn't imagine some editor saying to me: "Yes, Miss Pike, we love this children's book you've written, but I'm afraid we can't publish it. You see, we've heard that you can't play volleyball. We don't *pub*lish non-volleyball-playing writers." That wasn't *too* likely to happen.

So, in the *big* picture, none of this mattered. But right now, I was trapped inside the *little* picture. Trapped with a maniacal gym teacher, and a bunch of half-crazed volleyball players. Most of whom were boys.

Don't get me wrong. A lot of the girls were good players, but (except for Helen Gallway) they weren't out of their minds. If the ball came to them, they hit it over the net. They didn't knock anyone out of the way to get to it. And they didn't try to maim their opponents with the ball.

It was while I was in the middle of some of these thoughts that disaster struck. Actually, it was a volleyball that struck. It struck me, right in the face.

Whap! Ow! I didn't even see it coming. I felt as if I were in one of those cartoons in which the characters see stars when they get clobbered. The ball hit me in the left eye area. My nose, my eye, my left cheek! They stung like crazy.

"Are you okay?" asked Tom Harold, who had served the ball for the other team. "I didn't mean to hit you."

"No, I'm not okay!" I exploded, still holding my face. "My nose feels like it's broken!"

In a second, my pal Ms. Walden was back on the scene. "Pike, calm down. What's the matter?"

"That idiot smashed the ball right into my face," I shouted. I had completely lost my cool.

"Okay, there's no need to call names," Ms. Walden said to me crossly. "It was an accident. And maybe if you hadn't been daydreaming it wouldn't have happened."

I couldn't believe what I was hearing. She wasn't in the least concerned that my cheek might be fractured, or my nose broken. No, she was scolding me for getting hit.

She was crazy.

They were all crazy.

"Why don't *you* try getting slammed in the head with a volleyball!" I shouted at her.

Ms. Walden's face turned pink, then red, then crimson. "That's enough of your mouth, Pike!" she cried. "You are benched! I want you over there on the bleachers for the rest of the game!"

By now, as you might imagine, everyone — and I mean everyone — in the gym was looking at me. No one was playing volleyball. Even Mr. De Young was watching.

I tossed Ms. Walden an angry, defiant look as I walked toward the bleachers. The gym was dead quiet. I felt as if I were going to the gallows or something, the way everyone was so hushed and attentive. (At least I'd ironed my uniform for this big moment.)

Then, thankfully, Mr. De Young blew his whistle and the games resumed.

I sat in the bleachers and concentrated on not crying. I wasn't sure if the pain or the public humiliation was worse. From time to time, I caught sight of Jessi looking my way sympathetically. I couldn't return her gaze, though. If I did, I'd have cried for sure. And crying would have been too awful. Things were bad enough as they were. If I cried, I would have to change schools, because I could certainly never show my face at SMS again. No, crying was definitely out.

Staring at the ceiling was a good way not to cry. I did that until, eventually, the urge to cry passed. It was replaced by a feeling of great annoyance. Who did Ms. Walden think she was, anyway? Some sort of great gym goddess? *You are benched!* I mean, big deal, really. It wasn't exactly the worst torture on earth.

Ironically, this was what I had wanted. Clearly, I loathed volleyball. So to punish me, Ms. Walden tells me I can't play volleyball. It didn't make a whole lot of sense.

After about a zillion years, gym ended. "I'll be looking for a better attitude next class, Pike," Ms. Walden said to me as the kids emptied into the locker rooms. "How's your face?"

Like she really cared.

"Fine," I said in a voice I hope was cold. Truthfully, my cheek still stung, but I didn't feel like telling her that.

I had almost reached the locker room when Jessi caught up to me. "Are you okay?" she asked, putting her arm around my shoulder.

Biting my lip, I nodded. That awful crying feeling was coming back. I couldn't let it get the best of me.

When I got home from school that afternoon, all I wanted was to be alone. But that wasn't meant to be. No sooner had I walked through the door than my mother intercepted me. "Mal, could you hold the fort here for a little while?" she asked. This wasn't a real question. Both of us knew it. It was an order disguised as a question. My mother was pulling on her coat as she spoke. "I have to go get Margo at school."

"How come?"

"The nurse's office called. She threw up at

about two-thirty and they didn't want to let her walk home feeling sick."

"Poor Margo," I said.

"It's probably just a bug of some sort," said my mother as she hurried to the door.

The door had barely closed when I heard a banging, pounding sound. It was coming from the kitchen. With a sigh, I ran upstairs to see what was going on.

"Pass to me! Pass to me!" I heard Adam shout.

A basketball thudded off the wall in front of me. "What are you doing?" I yelled.

"What does it look like?" asked Jordan. The triplets and Nicky were breathless from playing ball.

"It looks like you're playing basketball in the house, which you're not allowed to do," I snapped.

"Bug off, Mallory!" said Jordan.

"You bug off!" I yelled back.

With the ball in my hands, I disappeared into my bedroom. Behind me I could hear the boys grumble, but I didn't care. I'd come to a decision. The only thing I disliked as much as sports was boys!

# CHAPTER 7

I've always tried to learn from my mistakes. On Thursday, Friday, and over the weekend, I considered everything that had gone wrong in gym on Wednesday. And I came up with a realization.

If I kept getting benched, I would never have to play volleyball.

There it was. The solution to my volleyball problem. It was so simple. I should have seen it immediately.

Of course, I know why I didn't see it. I'm generally considered to be a "good" kid. Being the oldest of eight has made me cooperative to an extreme. Being disruptive and ornery isn't my nature. I'm never in trouble in school. That day in gym was the first time I'd been singled out for a punishment.

But I'd survived. And it had been a lot less awful than playing volleyball with a bunch of boys.

I was onto a good thing, and I knew it.

All it would take was nerve. Lots of nerve. Did I have enough nerve? I wasn't sure. When Monday gym class rolled around, I still wasn't sure. I changed into my gym outfit and wandered onto the court, still debating whether I should just try to play the dumb game or if I should get myself benched.

The answer came to me in the form of Robbie Mara.

"Hey, Mallory, how's your face?" he asked as I tied on my pinny.

"It's all right."

"It doesn't hurt anymore?"

"No."

A big, goofy grin swept across his face. "That's strange," he said. "Because your face is killing me!"

Two guys nearby laughed and looked at me for my reaction. "That's very humorous, Robbie," I said dryly. "I think I first heard that joke in kindergarten."

He hadn't made me mad, just kind of disgusted. He was a moron. This game was for morons. And I wasn't going to play it. I simply turned and walked toward the bleachers, untying my pinny on the way.

"Pike!" Ms. Walden barked, following me across the gym. "What are you doing?"

"I'm benching myself," I told her.

"I don't think so," she said. "Get back onto that court."

"Sorry, Ms. Walden," I told her firmly. "I'm not playing."

Ms. Walden's eyes narrowed, but her cheeks only colored to that pink level of anger. "If you're not back on that court by the time Mr. De Young blows the whistle, you can count on detention."

"Fine," I said.

With that, Ms. Walden returned to the game. For a moment I almost caved in and ran onto the court. But the moment passed. Mr. De Young blew his whistle and still I sat on the bleacher.

Detention.

I'd never had it before. Naturally, I was old enough to know it wasn't the end of the world. Some kids spent half their lives in detention. They didn't seem to care after awhile.

Still, it was a blemish on my perfect no-detention record. In my usual, over-imaginative way, I wondered if this was the beginning of my slide into a life of crime. I could see the movie of my life story opening with me sitting in detention. The next scene was me sitting in a police station. Really, though, once you stopped caring about getting into trouble, where did you draw the line?

I'd have to worry about that later. Right

now, this was working out very well for me. No volleyball was the best reward anyone could give me.

It turned out that detention wasn't bad, either. I did my homework while I was there. Being "bad" was a breeze.

"Your parents will be receiving written notification of your detention," said Mr. Zizmore, the detention monitor, just as we were about to leave.

Written notification! Maybe detention wasn't a total breeze.

Suddenly I had a sinking feeling in the pit of my stomach. My parents would be shocked. And upset. I wouldn't be able to bear their worried, concerned faces. I didn't want to hear their lecture, either. Especially since I couldn't promise it would never happen again. I fully intended to avoid volleyball until the end of the unit. When something works, you stay with it.

As I stepped out of the detention classroom, I was deep in thought, worrying about this. That's why I almost ran right into Ben.

"Hi. What are you doing here?" I asked.

"Waiting for you," he said. "I thought maybe you'd be feeling bad. You know, like you might want to talk to someone or . . . you know. I heard what happened from a guy in my math class."

"It's big news, huh," I said sourly.

"Not really. It's just that he knows you and I are friends, so he mentioned it. Are you okay?"

"I guess so," I said as we walked down the hall. "But it has been a pretty rotten day. Now I have to worry about my parents finding out. The school is sending them a letter."

"Will they be angry?" he asked.

"A little, but mostly they'll be concerned. That's almost worse."

"I know what you mean," he agreed. "They'll look all crushed and sad. It's much worse. What started this, anyway?"

I filled him in on how much I hated volleyball and how Ms. Walden was picking on me. I left out the part about how annoying the boys are. I didn't feel right saying that to him since he is a boy.

Talking to Ben is so easy. He listens and always tries to understand. He even told me he isn't crazy about volleyball himself. "And playing with the girls *is* weird," he said. "I'm always afraid I'm going to step on them or something."

"That doesn't bother some boys," I said bitterly.

"Yeah, well, now that you've told me what happened to you, I'm going to play differently in gym class. I know girls aren't delicate little flowers or anything like that. But most of them don't play sports the same way boys do. They have a different style. It's just as good, but different."

Ben is so great.

It's hard to believe he's a boy.

We walked to my door and then stood around talking for awhile longer, until I suddenly realized what time it was. Detention had thrown me off schedule. I'd forgotten I was arriving home an hour later than usual. "Gosh!" I said. "I have to get ready for my Baby-sitter's Club meeting. Thanks for waiting for me."

"No problem."

"Ben," I said, "even though I'm glad you waited, you don't *have* to wait each time it happens."

A look of confusion swept over Ben's face. "It's going to happen again?"

"I'm afraid so," I said, sighing. "I'm *not* playing volleyball. I've made up my mind."

"Don't you think it would be simpler to play? I mean, just sort of grin and bear it. It won't last forever."

I shook my head. "No. I've made up my mind."

"I think you're making a mistake," said Ben.

"Maybe. But I'm still not playing volleyball."

Ben smiled sadly. "Then I'll wait for you to get out of detention every day until volleyball is over."

"You don't have to."

"It's okay," he said as he walked across the lawn. "See you tomorrow."

"See you," I said with a wave.

Turning to go into the house, I thought of something. The mail. I wondered if anyone had picked it up yet.

Before this, I hadn't paid a lot of attention to the mail. But now I had a reason to. It occurred to me that if that notice from the school had been in the mailbox right now — as it would be in a few days — I could simply take it out of the mailbox and stuff it into my pocket.

Then a pang of guilt hit me. I envisioned my face on a Most Wanted Poster in the post office. Mallory Pike: Wanted for Mail Fraud.

I pushed the thought aside. I wasn't going to descend into a life of crime. As Ben had said, it was only for a short while. This just had to be done.

From now on, I would be checking the mail daily.

# CHAPTER 8

TUESDAY

WHAT'S GOING ON AROUND HERE?
HAVE ALL THE KIDS IN STONEYBROOK
SUDDENLY TURNED INTO MONSTERS?
I'VE BEEN READING THE NOTEBOOK
AND EVERYONE SEEMS TO BE
HAVING A TOUGH TIME BABY-SITTING
LATELY. AND WITH KIDS WHO ARE
USUALLY PRETTY GOOD, TOO! WHAT
GIVES? I'M ASKING BECAUSE I HAD
AN AWFUL TIME TAKING CARE OF
HUNTER. I'VE NEVER SEEN MY BROTHER
BE SO FRUSTRATING.

Logan was right. The kids seemed to have turned into monsters. But he missed one detail that I noticed right away. All the kids who were being difficult were boys! (Logan probably missed this since he, himself, is a boy.)

Nine-year-old Kerry, Logan's sister, was as sweet as always. She hadn't changed. But five-year-old Hunter was like a wild child when Logan sat for him on Tuesday evening. First he threw his eight million Legos all over the living room floor and refused to pick them up. (Kerry picked them up for him.) Later, Hunter demanded that Logan make him a hamburger for supper, even though Mrs. Bruno had left a tuna casserole for Logan to heat up. Logan was nice enough to make the hamburger, but when it was ready, Hunter said it was salty and refused to eat it. (Kerry ate it for him and said it was delicious.)

While Kerry was angelically doing her homework in her room, Hunter was throwing a fit because he didn't want to brush his teeth before going to bed. Logan relented and said he didn't have to brush, but just getting Hunter into bed was a major accomplishment. He got up five times, wanting everything from water to a different Teddy bear to sleep with, before he finally nodded off.

Logan was exhausted by the time his parents returned home.

He told us all this when he came by for a Wednesday BSC meeting. He and Mary Anne had been studying together again that afternoon. I guess as long as he was around, he figured he might as well come to the meeting.

To tell the truth, I wasn't particularly happy to see him. I was still down on boys. And, nice as he is, Logan is a boy. The meetings are different when he's there, too. Everyone is quieter. We hardly ever giggle. It's as if we're trying to act more mature just because Logan is there.

Also, I must admit that I was in a crabby mood that day anyway. Since it was Wednesday, I had once again had gym. And I had benched myself again. And I had gotten detention again. All through detention I was looking forward to the BSC meeting as the only bright spot in my dismal day, and I didn't want a boy — not even Logan — interfering with that.

Anyway, like it or not, Logan was there and he told us about how tough Hunter had been to take care of. Everyone agreed with him that the kids have been especially difficult lately.

"The Rodowsky boys were wild yesterday," Claudia complained. (And normally Claudia likes them.) "They're *always* wild," she continued, "but yesterday Jackie locked Bo in the toolshed because he wanted to paint the inside of Bo's doghouse. Then he lost the key to the toolshed. Poor Bo was howling his head off. While I was fiddling in the lock with a bobby pin, he and Archie got into a fight. The next thing I knew, blue paint was flying everywhere. So Shea decided to play the big brother, saying *he'd* paint the doghouse. But he didn't realize Jackie had wanted to paint the inside, and he began slapping the paint on the outside — which caused another fight. And then Shea only painted half of the doghouse, got bored, and went to a friend's house."

"Oh, my gosh." Stacey laughed sympathetically. "What finally happened?"

"By the time Mrs. Rodowsky came back, I had cleaned up the boys, but Bo was still howling and the doghouse was still half blue."

"Was Mrs. Rodowsky mad?" asked Jessi.

Claudia shrugged. "She didn't look thrilled. Luckily she had an extra key for the toolshed."

"I know how you must have felt," Dawn said. "I had a tough time with the Barretts the other day. Buddy gave me the most trouble. He wouldn't stop picking on Suzi and Marnie."

"He was picking on Marnie?" exclaimed Mary Anne.

"Yeah. I couldn't believe it. Here was this big seven-year-old annoying this little toddler. And he wouldn't stop. He kept taking away her toys, and he turned off her *Sesame Street* video so he could watch his own cartoons. He was worse with Suzi. Of course, being four, she fights back, but she's no match for him. At one point I actually had to threaten to call his mother."

As I listened to all the stories, I wondered if I should point out the fact which was so blaringly obvious to me. The girls we sat for were behaving just fine. It was the boys who were horrible. Ordinarily I would have just come out and said it, but I hesitated because I didn't want to offend Logan.

Finally I decided to speak up, though. Logan would just have to face the facts.

"Hasn't anyone else noticed that we're only having trouble with the boys?" I asked.

"That's not so," said Mary Anne. "Is it?"

"You know, Mal *is* right," said Kristy. "I wonder why that's happening."

"Could we be favoring the girls without meaning to?" Stacey ventured. "Maybe that's making the boys act up so they can get attention."

"I don't think so," said Claudia. "There are no girls in the Rodowsky family."

"Still," Kristy said pensively. "Maybe we should be extra nice to the boys and see what happens."

"I was nice to Buddy Barrett, and it didn't make a bit of difference," Dawn disagreed.

"I don't think I was favoring Becca over Squirt, either," said Jessi. "She was just being good and he was a terror."

"Logan, you're a boy. Do you have any ideas about this?" Stacey asked.

Logan shook his head. "Not really. All I can think of is that boys are worse at some ages and girls are worse at other ages. Maybe we have a bunch of boys at bad ages."

"Or maybe it's just a coincidence," Jessi volunteered.

"I know," said Dawn, smiling. "The planets are in some strange alignment that affects boys only."

"That's pretty doubtful," said Logan. "I haven't been acting strangely."

"That's a matter of opinion," teased Mary Anne.

Logan responded in typical boy fashion by jabbing Mary Anne in the arm with his knuckles. Mary Anne pretended it hurt, but she was laughing.

"I know what the problem is," I spoke up. "The problem is that boys are pains and girls are not. We just never noticed it before."

"Thanks a lot," Logan said, only half laughing.

"I'm sorry, Logan. But that's how it seems to me," I replied.

"What about Ben?" Dawn asked.

"Ben is different," I replied.

"So is Logan, then," Mary Anne said, taking Logan's hand.

"Wait a minute," Logan objected. "Ben and I aren't the only two decent guys in the world. There are lots of nice guys."

"I agree," said Stacey. "I don't think your theory holds up, Mal."

"Maybe, maybe not," I said. "I'm just saying how it seems to me."

At that moment the phone rang. It was Dr. Johanssen. She needed someone to sit for Charlotte for a few hours the next day. "One girl, no brothers, the perfect client," I said. "I'll take the job, if no one else wants it."

Everyone else was busy, so I did wind up taking the job. Honestly, I don't know if I would have volunteered for the job if Charlotte had been a boy. Boys were nothing but trouble!

After a few more calls, the meeting ended. Jessi and I walked outside together. "Why are you so down on boys lately?" Jessi asked me.

"I'm just making observations," I told her.

"What I see is that boys are a pain. Look at the evidence!"

"I don't know," she said, shaking her head. "Didn't Ben wait for you after detention again today? That's not being a pain. That's pretty sweet, if you ask me."

"I said Ben was different, didn't I? He's the exception that proves the rule."

Jessi laughed lightly. "I think you're just annoyed at boys because we have to play volleyball with them."

"But the boys love to play volleyball, so that proves it!" I cried. "Only people who are pains at heart could love such a dumb game."

"For a sensible person, you can be really illogical sometimes," said Jessi. "Besides, I kind of like volleyball."

I clamped my hands over my ears. "I didn't hear that," I said.

"But I do," Jessi insisted.

I took my hands from my ears and put them on Jessi's shoulders. "No. You may think you like volleyball, but you're mistaken. You're stressed. Or perhaps you've been stepped on and smacked with the ball too many times. It's affected your brain. Go home. Get a good night's sleep. You'll come to your senses in the morning."

# CHAPTER 9

Finally, my luck seemed to be changing —
at least in the baby-sitting department. Sitting
for Charlotte Johanssen on Thursday was a
breeze. She was good as gold. But, of course,
she *is* a girl.

Then, at the Friday BSC meeting, Mrs. Hobart called. I took the job she offered because
Ben's three brothers are such great kids. Still,
I was nervous. What if they were suddenly
transformed like all the other formerly good
boys? I decided to risk it, though.

As it turned out, the three of them were
fine. Better than fine. Angels! That fact is even
more amazing since it was a cold, rainy day
and they were cooped up inside the house.

When six-year-old Mathew asked if we
could make chocolate chip cookies, I drew in
a deep breath. Cooking with kids can be a
disaster if they decide not to cooperate. I didn't
want to end up like Jessi, cleaning the entire

kitchen. I said no, but the kids wouldn't give up.

"Please, please, please," begged four-year-old Johnny. "There's nothing to do."

"Our mom won't mind," eight-year-old James pressed. "She's been promising and promising to make them, but she never has the time. The chocolate chips are right in the cabinet. I can find them." Before I could object, he was digging through the cabinet and soon produced the chips, as well as flour, sugar, and a bottle of vanilla extract.

At the same time, Mathew was hunting through the refrigerator for eggs and milk. Obviously, the boys had baked cookies before. It was pretty hard to say no to them.

So, even though it was against my better judgment, we began making chocolate chip cookies. And guess what. We had a great time!

We baked some regular round cookies, and then we made some in different shapes. Each boy made one in the shape of his first initial. We even made a B cookie for Ben. He was at school that afternoon at a special meeting of the school paper.

As I watched the boys molding their cookies, I wondered why they were so different from other boys. That's when I came up with my second big theory.

Ben and his brothers are from Australia!

That's why they were different. Maybe not all boys were pains, just American boys.

Then I thought of Logan. I had to admit he wasn't a pain, either. But he's from Kentucky. And he hasn't been in Stoneybrook all that long. At least not long enough to turn into a pain.

So, here was my new theory: American boys from Stoneybrook were the biggest pains on earth.

There must be something about Stoneybrook that made boys particularly obnoxious. Look at my brothers. They've lived here all their lives and they were the ultimate pains. Was it the water? The school system? The teams they played on?

I knew! It was gym!

Kids take gym from kindergarten on up. There must be something in the way Stoneybrook teachers conduct the boys' gym classes that made boys think they could do anything they pleased. It was a pretty clear connection. The teachers encourage them to play as if winning were the most important thing in the world. I wasn't sure exactly what it was, but something in the way they teach the boys gym was encouraging them to be incredible twerps.

But what about the little boys? They weren't taking gym yet. They must have been under the influence of the older boys. The little guys couldn't help but pick it up.

As farfetched as this theory might sound, the more I thought about it, the more it made sense. The most revolting subject on earth — gym — would naturally produce the most revolting people on earth — boys.

Girls take gym, of course. But it isn't the same. Most girls didn't seem to me to be as serious about gym as boys were. There's probably only one girls sports event for every five the boys have. Take something like basketball: The girls have a team. But only a few kids and one or two parents come to the games. When the boys' team has a game, the benches are full.

That makes boys feel they're more important. And feeling more important must make them obnoxious.

I was glad that, at least, this wasn't a worldwide syndrome. Stoneybrook was simply the worst offender. That left some hope. When I was older, I could move to some place (like Australia or Kentucky) where the boys act more like human beings.

I pondered these things as the cookies baked and the boys helped me clean up the kitchen. When the cookies were done we let them cool a moment, just long enough to pour ourselves big glasses of milk. Then James looked at the clock and saw that it was time for a movie he wanted to watch on TV. It was *Return of the Master Killer*, one of those martial arts movies. We took our cookies and milk into the den and turned on the movie.

It was time for me to worry again. My brothers love these fighting movies, too. The minute one comes on, they're up, kicking, shouting, karate-chopping the air, right along with the guys in the movie. One of my brothers (usually Nicky or Byron) always gets hurt before the movie ends.

But I was in luck again. The Hobart boys were crazy about the movie, but they showed their enthusiasm by shouting things like: "Good one!" "Go, get him!" "All right!" Not by knocking over lamps and belting one another in the mouth as my brothers would have done.

We were an hour into the movie when Ben came home. "*Return of the Master Killer*, huh?" he said, standing in the doorway. "I like this one, but not as much as *A Slice of Death*. That's my favorite."

"*Master Killer* is way better," James disagreed.

"I smell cookies," Ben observed.

"Should we give him his special cookie?" I asked the guys.

"You can give it to him," said Mathew, his eyes glued to the screen.

Ben and I walked into the kitchen and I gave him his B cookie.

"It looks like the monsters weren't being too bad for you," said Ben as he bit into the cookie.

"Bad?" I cried. "They're wonderful. You're so lucky."

Ben laughed. "It must be you. They're not always so wonderful."

"Whenever I see them, they are. They're angels!"

"Ha!" Ben hooted. "They may look like angels, but believe me, they're not."

"I don't believe you," I insisted. "I would give anything to trade brothers with you."

"No you wouldn't."

"I'm serious. I would."

"You'd be sorry." Ben laughed.

"You're the one who would be sorry. If you got my brothers it would be like a bomb hit your house. You know what they're like."

"They're not so terrible," said Ben, reaching for another cookie.

"Not so terrible!" I shrieked. "How can you say that?"

Ben just laughed.

"Ben," I said, "what's gym like in Australia?"

He looked at me, surprised. "I don't know.

Kind of like it is here. In my school we only had it once a week, though."

"See! I knew it!" I cried.

"Knew what?"

"Nothing. Nothing. It's just a theory I'm working on," I told him.

"Speaking of gym," he said seriously. "Did that detention notice ever come to your house?"

I nodded. "I grabbed it before anyone saw it. I have another one in my pocket right now. I got it out of the mailbox before I came over today. In the nick of time, too. My mother came outside and saw me looking through the mail. Luckily I had just stuck the letter in my jacket pocket. It was a close call."

"Mal, why don't you just play volleyball? It's better than lying to your parents," Ben said with a sigh.

"I'm not lying to them," I protested.

Ben cocked his head and looked at me like he wasn't buying my excuse.

"I'm not! I'm just sparing them from being upset."

"Well, do what you like," he said. "But I think there's going to be trouble if they find out. Besides that, once you get on bad terms with a teacher, he — or she — can make your life miserable. *And*, the mark is going to appear on your report card. What are you going to say when your parents ask why you failed gym?"

I turned pale. Fail gym! I hadn't thought of that. I've never failed a subject in my life. Would I have to go to summer school? For *gym*? What a perfect way to ruin a summer.

"Gosh, I hadn't thought about all that," I admitted, slumping onto a kitchen chair, my head in my hands. "It sounds like you've been thinking about it a lot."

"Sure. Well, I think about *you* a lot."

"Yeah?"

"Sure."

"Okay," I said. "Monday I'm going to play volleyball."

"Good," said Ben, smiling. "I think that's a great idea."

I sighed. "I'll try, anyhow."

# CHAPTER 10

On Monday I entered gym class with the very best of intentions. Really. I did.

"Are you going to play?" Jessi gasped as I walked out toward my teammates.

"Yes," I replied, chin up, eyes straight ahead.

"Good for you," she said. "You'll be great."

"Thanks, but I'll settle for being alive when this is over."

With an encouraging pat on the shoulder, Jessi ran off to her team.

"To what do we owe this honor?" asked Helen Gallway as I tied on my pinny.

I gave her a tight little smile and said nothing.

Robbie Mara exchanged a quick glance with another boy on the team, Noah Fein. Noah rolled his eyes and threw up his hands. "We're doomed," he muttered.

I really couldn't blame my teammates for

not being thrilled about my return. I think they may actually have won a couple of games while I was on the bleachers. But I couldn't worry about that. I was supposed to play, and I was going to play. That's all there was to it.

Ms. Walden noticed me, but she didn't say anything. Soon Mr. De Young blew his whistle and the game started. I don't know if it was intentional, but the girl serving on the other side gave me a break. She didn't send the ball directly to me. I was able to get away with looking like I was paying attention, hopping lightly on the balls of my feet with my hands half up in the air as if I were prepared to — even hoping to — slap the ball at any moment. (Truthfully, my hands were poised to cover my head in case the ball came flying at it. But no one else had to know that.)

If the game had continued that way, everything would have been fine. But it didn't.

Chris Brooks came up to serve for the other team. He looked at me and remembered the one bright idea he'd probably ever had in his life. (I imagined him thinking in caveman talk: "Hit ball to Mallory. Win game.")

In minutes, I felt like a character in a video game, one who has to keep darting and leaping to avoid being pulverized by some cosmic blast. Chris pounded serve after serve directly at me. I wanted to return the ball, but I couldn't. I'm sorry, it just goes against human nature — at least *my* human nature — not to duck when a flying object is heading straight at you.

It was so demoralizing! It wasn't fair that I was under attack like this. The grunts and groans of my teammates didn't help. I felt bad enough about being such a clod. Having to deal with their annoyance just made me feel worse. I was sorry I was letting them down. But they could have had a little sympathy for what I was going through. *They* weren't being bombarded with a volleyball, after all. I was the one under attack.

Someone could have said, "Hey, leave her alone, Chris!" But no. They yelled: "Come on, Mallory!" "Don't just stand there!" "Hit it!" (Maybe they felt they had to fill in for Ms. Walden since she wasn't there at the moment to torment me.)

Then came the last straw. "We *were* winning," said Helen, groaning loudly. Then she sighed as if she couldn't bear the pain of losing at volleyball.

That was all I could take. "Listen, Helen," I snapped, untying my pinny. "You don't have to worry anymore. Win your idiotic game. I'm leaving!"

Throwing my pinny on the ground (and

stepping on it just for good measure), I stomped over to the bleachers.

I'd tried. But it hadn't worked. Volleyball and I simply weren't a match. There was no way I was willing to subject myself to it for another minute.

After about thirty seconds on the bench, Ms. Walden was by my side. Today she took a different approach with me. Instead of biting my head off, she sat down beside me.

"Okay, Pike. Let's talk about this. What, exactly, is bugging you?"

Looking down, I tried to think of a way to explain. But all I could do was notice how white Ms. Walden's sneakers were. And what thick ankles she had.

"Pike! I asked you a question," Ms. Walden pressed.

"I can't play volleyball, and I don't see why I should have to," was all I could think to say.

"Maybe if you tried, you'd learn how to play."

"I just did try," I said, trying not to sound too disrespectful. "It didn't work."

"Quitting isn't going to get you anywhere in life," said Ms. Walden. "This is a bad pattern. First you quit at volleyball, next thing you know, you'll be quitting college if it gets tough. Or you'll be quitting jobs you don't like. I'm telling you, don't start this quitting stuff now. Life eats up quitters."

Okay. I know that, in theory, what she said was true. Quitting is not a good habit to get into. But I'm not a quitter! I've done lots of difficult things in my life.

I simply could not play volleyball.

It drives me crazy that sports people think life is like sports. Life is not sports! Life is life and sports is sports.

Ms. Walden's telling me that I would end up some huge failure in life just because I didn't want to play volleyball made me even madder and crabbier than I already was. "I'm not playing volleyball, Ms. Walden," I said calmly. "I don't care what you do to me. I'll go to detention every afternoon if I have to. But I'm not playing."

"What do your parents say about this?" she asked.

I studied her sneakers. Did she have some secret for keeping them so white? Did she have many pairs? Maybe she threw her sneakers out the minute they got smudged and bought new ones.

"Your parents, Pike! What do they think of this?"

"They say it's okay," I lied. "They don't think I should have to play if I don't want to."

"Is that so?" Ms. Walden muttered. Then, without another word, she stood up and walked back to the volleyball games.

Now I was really confused. Had I won? Was she going to leave me alone? She hadn't mentioned detention or anything.

When gym ended, I headed for the locker. "Just a minute, Pike," Ms. Walden called, approaching me. "Instead of detention today, I have a different idea. See those pinnies?" She pointed to the pile of colored cloth that was growing as the girls filed by, each throwing her pinny on. "I want you to come by after school and pick them up. The boys' pinnies, too. They have to be washed. You can use the washing machine in the home ec room."

My jaw dropped. This was inhuman.

"But . . . but . . ." I stammered. It was no use. Before I could get any more words out, Ms. Walden was on her way into the locker room.

"What happened?" Jessi asked, from behind me.

"I have to wash all those stinky pinnies this afternoon," I said, still stunned by the news.

"Pew." She looked at me sympathetically. "I'd stay and help you, but I have a ballet class this afternoon."

"That's okay," I told her as we trotted into the locker room. "It's not the end of the world."

That's what I said. But when I was standing in the home ec room with a reeking, steaming, pile of sweat-stained pinnies, I decided the end of the world might have been preferable. They were so stinky I didn't even want to touch them.

"I'll be in the classroom across the way, doing some paperwork," Ms. Walden told me. "Keep this door open."

I'm sure she would have claimed she wanted the door open for safety reasons. I think it was really part of her scheme to punish me, though. As I stood there tossing pinnies into the machine, everyone who passed by could see me. Since it's not usual to see someone doing wash in the home ec room after school *everyone* looked in.

With my head down, I pretended to be unaware of the kids gawking at me. And I was able to do some homework while the machine ran through its cycles. After a while, I had a bunch of clean but soaking wet pinnies. I began throwing them into the dryer.

When I looked up, I was face to face with a bunch of boys hanging in the doorway. Apparently they had been watching me work and were getting a huge kick out of it.

One of them was Robbie Mara. "Hey, Mallory. Don't get pinny-washer's elbow," he teased. "You wouldn't want to throw off your volleyball game."

"Ha, ha," I said with as much disdain in my voice as possible.

"Yeah!" Noah Fein chimed in. "It would break Chris Brooks's heart. He wouldn't have anybody to smash with the ball."

"Get lost, jerks," I muttered.

That just made them laugh. "Hey, Mal, don't fall into the washing machine!" Tom Harold called as the boys moved on. "But maybe you should go soak your head. It might help."

Yuck. Sports and Stoneybrook boys. I couldn't think of any two things I hated more!

# CHAPTER 11

Saturday

Last week I thought Mal was a little crazy when she was griping about boys. Now I'm not so sure. Over the weekend I sat for David Michael, Emily Michelle, Andrew and Karen. Emily and Karen were angels. David Michael and Andrew were devils! Really, Mal's theory doesn't make a lot of sense. Still...

There's no arguing with evidence. And the evidence against boys was mounting. That's what Kristy discovered when she sat for her younger brothers and sisters.

Watson and Kristy's mom were going to some fancy black-tie awards dinner and they'd invited Nannie along. Kristy's older brothers were both busy, so Kristy was left in charge.

Since Karen and Andrew only live at their father's every other weekend, Kristy was glad to spend time with them. She was looking forward to an evening of playing board games, popping popcorn, and telling jokes. That's not what happened, though.

Emily Michelle, who you might expect to be the problem since she's so little, was great. She sat on the floor, stacking blocks or playing with her current favorite game, Shark Attack. (Emily doesn't really know how to play but she likes to fool around with the game pieces.) Karen, who adores Kristy, decided to be her baby-sitting helper.

But Andrew and David Michael acted like . . . like *boys*. David Michael hogged the TV. He insisted on watching *G.I. Joe* videos and threw a fit when Kristy insisted that he let Emily watch *The Care Bears*. After sulking, he dragged out his small plastic jets and began flying them across the family room.

"Stop it!" Kristy cried as a jet skidded off the top of the TV and crashed into the wall.

David Michael didn't listen. He was still mad about losing control of the TV. He hurled another plastic jet over Kristy's head.

"That's enough!" Kristy shouted, pulling the jets from his hands. "I think you better — "

She didn't get a chance to finish her sentence. A blood-curdling scream from Emily Michelle stopped her cold. Andrew had taken away Shark Attack, which she was playing with while watching *The Care Bears*.

"She doesn't play it right," Andrew whined. "She's too little to play this game."

"That's okay. She likes it anyway. Give it back to her," said Kristy.

Andrew sat down in a huff. "I'm going to show her how to play it right." This involved setting up the pieces and scolding Emily every time she grabbed for one of them. "No, Emily, you're doing it wrong!" he'd shout.

"Just give it back to her. Please," said Kristy.

"No! I'm showing her," Andrew insisted angrily.

Kristy slid the game away from him and back in front of Emily. "She doesn't want to be shown," Kristy told him. "She was happy playing the game her own way."

Andrew stood up and stomped out of the

room. "Her own way is stupid!"

"Emily is little," Kristy called after him. "She doesn't know how to — "

Again, Kristy was cut off. Her attention was diverted back to David Michael who had taken a tape player off a shelf and begun playing it at top volume. "Turn that down!" Kristy yelled over the noise.

"I want to drown out the Care Bears," he said. "I can't stand the way those characters talk."

"Turn it down or take it to your room," Kristy told him.

"No," said David Michael. "I have as much right to be here as anyone else."

Kristy turned it down *for* him.

David Michael turned it back up.

Kristy turned it down.

David Michael wrenched the box away and turned it to full volume.

Kristy pulled it back and took out the batteries. "Give me those!" David Michael shouted, grabbing at the batteries Kristy held.

Finally, Kristy took the batteries and threw them out the window into the yard.

The rest of the evening was no better. Andrew and David Michael were like a terror tag team. While one gave Kristy trouble, the other thought up new ways to make more trouble.

By the time the adults got home all the kids

were asleep — including Kristy who had conked out on the couch. She said she couldn't remember ever being so tired or frazzled in her life.

Kristy told us this story at our Monday afternoon meeting. I sat on Claudia's rug, listening, glad to hear about somebody else's troubles. It stopped me from thinking about my own. And I sure had enough of them to think about.

That afternoon I'd finished washing the pinnies at about four-thirty. I was in such a hurry to get home for the BSC meeting that I almost forgot to check the mailbox to make sure it didn't hold a detention notice.

I was halfway up the stairs when I turned back for the mail. My heart almost stopped. There was no mail. The box was empty.

Maybe there was just no mail today, I told myself hopefully. And even if there had been mail, there might not have been a detention notice.

By five o'clock, I had almost convinced myself there was nothing to worry about. I'd changed my clothes and was running a brush through my hair when my mother walked into my room. One look at her face told me that the worst had happened. The detention notice had arrived.

Mom sat on my bed. "Mallory, what's this all about?" she asked, spreading the letter out on my quilt. "It says this is the third time you've been to detention."

"Today makes four," I admitted dismally. "You'll be getting that notice in the mail in a few days."

"What is going on?" she asked.

I sighed and plopped down on the bed. It was time to tell her the story. "And so," I said as I finished up, "it's like I'm under attack. Ms. Walden yells at me, the kids on the other team try to cream me with the ball just so they can win. It's horrible. And today Ms. Walden made me wash all the stupid pinnies . . . and some boys stopped to watch and were making fun of me and . . ." My voice cracked, and the next thing I knew I was crying.

Mom put her arm around me, which only made me cry harder, but it felt good. I hadn't wanted to admit, even to myself, how much these last two weeks had upset me. It seemed easier to act tough. But I was surprised at how good it felt to tell her; how good it felt to cry.

"This really is a problem, isn't it?" Mom said seriously. I brushed away my tears and checked to see if she was kidding me. She wasn't.

Mom and I sat on the bed together, thinking. "Maybe you could try talking to Ms. Walden," Mom suggested. "Ask her if one of the other kids could give you some pointers."

"She'd probably assign Helen Gallway," I said with a groan.

"You don't have to love Helen Gallway," Mom said. "Just let her give you some help. And maybe she could ask the other team to give you a break."

"She wouldn't do that. Anyway, it's mostly Chris Brooks who's the problem," I said.

"Could you talk to him?" Mom asked.

"I don't know him, really. I suppose I could try."

"Give it a shot," said Mom. "Then come back and tell me how it goes. If it doesn't work, we'll think of something else."

"Thanks, Mom," I said as she stood up.

"Sometimes we have to do things we don't like, Mal," she said. "Unfortunately, it's just part of life. Usually it's better not to run away from those things — although there are times when we'd like to."

"What things would you like to run away from?" I asked.

My mother smiled grimly. "Right now, I'd like to run away from making dinner, but it has to be done." She picked the paper off the bed. "And I don't want to see any more of these. Understand?"

"I understand," I said.

So, by the time I reached the BSC meeting I'd had an exhausting day. I was glad to sit back and listen to everyone else talk.

"I've been thinking about this boy thing a lot," said Claudia. "What could be causing it?"

"It's just a coincidence," Stacey said confidently. "It's like cards. You have a run of bad luck, then you have a run of good luck. It's mathematical, in a way."

"Leave it to our resident math whiz to see the problem in terms of math." Dawn laughed.

"But it is a math problem," Stacey insisted. "It has to do with odds and statistics."

"Statistics?" Jessi repeated.

"Yeah. Mr. Zizmore was talking about it today in class. Statistics can't always be trusted. Say, for example, a scientist surveys only people who support his theory and excludes people who don't support it. Then he could say one hundred percent of all people interviewed think this, but really he's only included in the survey the people who think a certain way to begin with."

"I get it. I think," said Claudia. "But what does that have to do with boys?"

"It means that we've come up with a theory that boys are a problem, but we're only looking at the cases in which they *are* a problem. I mean, look at the good time Mallory had sitting for the Hobart boys. And the other day. I sat for the Kormans. Bill was fine. And

Dawn, you sat for Norman Hill. He was okay, right?"

"Yeah, he was," Dawn admitted.

"See? They don't fit into our theory, so we're not talking about them. We're skewing the statistics, as Mr. Zizmore would say," Stacey concluded.

"That does make a lot of sense," said Kristy.

Maybe, I thought. Stacey made it sound very convincing. But I wasn't convinced. I liked my theory better. Boys from Stoneybrook had had their minds warped by gym class and were the weirdest creatures on earth. Now that was a theory which made sense to me.

After the meeting, Jessi asked me how the pinny-washing had gone. I told her the whole story, including the part about my mother finding the detention notice. "Wow," she said. "You're having some bad day."

"I was glad to talk to Mom, though," I told her. "She had some good ideas. But I don't know if they'll work."

"Ben was looking for you after school," Jessi said. "He wanted to hear how gym went."

"Did you tell him?"

"No. I figured you'd want to tell him yourself."

I looked across the street at Ben's house. "I'm going to go see if he's at home," I said to Jessi. "See you tomorrow."

Jessi waved good-bye as I crossed the street.

Ben answered the Hobarts' door. "Hi," he said, letting me in. "How did it go today?"

"Not so good," I replied, and told my story again.

"Robbie Mara is such a jerk," Ben said sympathetically when I got to the part where the boys teased me in the home ec room.

As I finished my story, Johnny, James, and Mathew came into the living room. They greeted me happily. "What are you guys up to?" I asked.

"We have to clean our rooms tonight," Mathew said. "They haven't been cleaned in two days."

"Two days!" I cried, impressed. "My brothers haven't cleaned their rooms in two months!"

"Boy, I wish I lived at your house," said Johnny.

"I wish you did, too." I laughed. "I'd love to trade brothers with Ben."

"You keep saying that, Mal, but I don't think you'd really want to," said Ben.

"I'm not kidding," I insisted.

"Let's do it then," said Ben. "Let's trade brothers."

"If only we could."

"We can. For one night, anyway. You send

your brothers here, and I'll send my brothers to your house."

"Yeah! Cool!" cried James.

"It's a deal!" I said. "I'll have one whole evening of peace and quiet in my house. It's going to be great!"

# CHAPTER 12

The Brother Switch was on! That Wednesday the schools were closed for a teacher's conference, so Tuesday night seemed the perfect night to try out the switch. (I didn't want to stick Mrs. Hobart with the job of getting my brothers off to school. That was asking too much!)

At first my parents thought the idea was strange. "Why are you doing this?" my father asked that night at the dinner table when I brought up the idea.

"Ben and I thought it would be an interesting experiment," I said. It didn't seem wise to tell the whole truth — that I also wanted to get rid of my brothers for a night. My parents might not have appreciated it, and it was certain to make my brothers uncooperative.

As it was, they loved the idea. "Yipeee! Mrs. Hobart is a great cook!" Nicky cried happily.

(My mother shot him a Look, but he didn't notice.)

"They have Game Boy, too," said Adam, who had been complaining lately that we didn't have enough Nintendo games.

"And no sisters to bug us for one whole night!" Jordan yelled jubilantly.

This time my sisters and I were the ones giving the Looks. "Bug you!" Vanessa cried. "*You* bug *us*!" (I was glad she said it, so I didn't have to.)

"We do not," Jordan objected. "You're always bugging us." He scrunched up his face and imitated a girl's high voice. "Stop it! Get out of here! You're making a mess! You're too loud! Ew, that's disgusting!"

"You *are* messy and disgusting!" said Margo.

"*You* are!" Nicky replied.

"That's enough," my father interrupted. "So. I take it you guys want to go to the Hobarts' tomorrow."

The question was answered with resounding cries of enthusiasm. So, still looking a bit uncertain about the plan, my mother called Mrs. Hobart after supper. From what I could make of their conversation, Mrs. Hobart was equally baffled by this idea, but she said it was okay by her.

After school the next day, I walked over to the Hobarts' with Nicky and the triplets. Then I walked back to my house with James, Mathew, and Johnny, sure I was getting the best of the deal — dumping off four monsters and returning with three little gentlemen. It was too good to be true. I almost felt guilty. Almost.

"Here we are," I said, letting the boys in the front door. Margo, Vanessa, and Claire were bunched up on the stairs, staring and giggling at them.

"These are my sisters," I said. "You'll get used to them."

Mom walked in from the kitchen and greeted the Hobarts. "Mal, take them upstairs and show them the boys' room."

"Good idea," I said, heading for the stairs. My sisters scrambled up ahead of us, still giggling. I stood aside and let the boys pass.

"This was your idea. You're in charge," my mother warned as the boys ran upstairs.

"No problem," I assured her. "You're going to love these kids, Mom. They're like angels."

Then I ran up the stairs after the boys.

"Bunk beds! Cooler than cool!" I heard James yell happily, when he reached the boys' room. When I reached the room, I was a little surprised to see the boys climbing over the beds as if they were a jungle gym.

"We've always wanted bunk beds," Mathew explained.

"Pick whichever bed you like," I told them.

That was a mistake. All three of them wanted the top bunk. Since there were only two tops, that presented a problem. Being the youngest, Johnny got stuck with the bottom. I felt bad for him, but figured it might be safer to leave him on the bottom. Still, this put Johnny in a pouty mood.

"Come on down to the rec room," I said to the boys.

Mathew's eyes lit up as if it were Christmas. "You have a room that you're allowed to wreck?"

"No, not wreck like that," I said. "Rec as in short for recreation." I was talking to myself, though. The boys raced down the hall and down the stairs, eager to find this room they could wreck.

And they did.

They found it and they wrecked it.

My sisters helped a lot. They introduced the boys to the joys of bouncing on the furniture. Claire turned into a super clown — making faces, doing silly dances, pretending to be a dog and barking at everyone. The other kids became giddy and silly. Soon they were all barking and growling at one another.

110

I sat on the stairs and watched this in stunned silence. What was going on? My angelic sisters meet the angelic Hobarts, and chaos breaks loose! This wasn't what was supposed to happen. I realized I better step in.

"Hey," I said, "how about playing Operation?" I figured that game was something that would occupy them — quietly.

"Okay," Vanessa agreed, dragging the game out from under the couch.

"Oh, man! Operation!" James cried. "I've always wanted to play this."

Bunk beds and Operation. So far James's visit to our house was turning out to be a dream come true — for him.

Soon the kids were happily playing Operation. I left them alone and went upstairs to the kitchen. "I'm going to run to the store and pick up a few things I need for supper," Mom said to me. "Do you think you can handle things for about an hour?"

"Sure. They're playing a game downstairs," I told her. Mom left and I spread my school books out on the kitchen table. I wanted to finish my homework so I could enjoy my day off tomorrow. (I felt like writing the principal a letter thanking him for picking a perfect day to have a teachers' conference. Wednesday! It meant I wouldn't have gym again until next Monday. Good choice, Mr. Taylor.)

I began my English assignment and became pretty engrossed in it. After about forty-five minutes I decided I'd better check on the kids. I suddenly realized it was *too* quiet.

When I entered the rec room, I sucked in my breath. The kids were gone and the place was . . . a wreck.

Chairs were stacked on top of the couch, the Ping-Pong table was on its side, the stools were upside down with the throw cover of a chair draped over them. It looked as if the kids had been trying to build some kind of furniture city. Games pieces were everywhere — Operation bones, Monopoly money and cards, pieces from the game Mousetrap.

Then I heard it.

The sound of water running.

I raced upstairs to the bathroom. The peels of hysterical laughter and high-pitched giggles that I heard while I was on the steps gave me a sinking feeling that something not-allowed was going on.

When I reached the top of the stairs, I saw the kids running back and forth between the bedrooms and the bathroom. They were soaking wet and covered with strings of pink soap foam. The hallway was covered with puddles.

You wouldn't believe what I found in the bathroom. The tub was almost overflowing and Claire stood in it with her clothes on, shooting whoever came in with the can of foam. She zapped me as I stepped into the room.

"I'm the foam-head silly-billy-goo-goo monster!" she cried gleefully as I turned off the water.

"Vanessa!" I screamed, lifting Claire out of the tub.

Sheepishly, Vanessa stuck her soaking wet, foam-flecked head into the bathroom. Yes?"

"How old are you? Two?" I shouted angrily. "Somebody could have gotten hurt, especially Claire. And look at this place. It's a mess!"

"We were going to clean it up," Vanessa replied huffily.

"How about starting with the rec room, then," I suggested as I peeled off Claire's shirt.

"The boys mostly did that," said Margo, sticking her head in beside Vanessa. "They thought we should play the Operation game in a pretend hospital."

"I don't care what they thought," I snapped. "Go get dried off and clean everything up."

Despite my big words, I wound up doing most of the work. If I'd left it to the kids it would never have been done before my mother got home.

Suppertime was all right, if you didn't mind a lot of giggling, poking, and under-the-table kicks. "Angels, huh?" my mother said skeptically as we cleared the table.

"I don't know what's with them tonight," I replied honestly. "It must be Vanessa, Margo, and Claire. The girls are making them nutso."

"It looks like the other way around to me," said my father as he dried a frying pan.

Things did not improve as the night wore on. None of the kids wanted to go to bed. But finally, everyone was settled in. My parents were downstairs watching TV and I was in my room reading.

Vanessa was on her bed reading, too. She got up to go to the bathroom. Ten minutes later I heard the sounds of shouts and giggles coming from the boys' room. When I checked on them, I found a full-fledged pillow fight being waged, with kids standing on top of dressers, jumping off the bunks, and darting in and out of closets.

"Go to sleep!" I shouted at them.

"We're having a slumber party," James told me.

"No, you're not," I said. "Claire, Margo, Vanessa, back to bed!"

I read for another fifteen minutes until I noticed that once again Vanessa had disappeared. That time I found her, and the rest of the kids, sitting in the dark. James held a flashlight under his face and was telling a scary story.

"Come on," I said. "Johnny and Claire will

have nightmares. Besides, you're supposed to be sleeping."

Margo made a face at me and stuck out her tongue.

I stuck out my tongue back at her.

Next thing I knew, all the kids were glaring and sticking their tongues out at me.

I never thought I'd say it, but I couldn't wait for the Hobart boys to go home!

# CHAPTER 13

The longest night in human history finally ended.

At about eleven-thirty, after stern words from my mother, and a special intimidating appearance by my father, everyone finally went to sleep. Half an hour later, Claire was up crying. Just as I predicted, the stories had scared her and she was having nightmares. No sooner was she asleep again, than I heard Johnny roaming the hall, whimpering. When I got out of bed to see what was wrong, he told me Mathew kept rolling around in the bunk above him and he couldn't sleep. We went downstairs and drank warm milk together until he yawned and felt sleepy enough to go back to bed. By then it was almost twelve-thirty.

At around three in the morning, I sat bolt upright. I'd been awakened by a loud thud. I met my parents and my sisters in the hall.

They'd heard it, too. It had come from the boys' room. We rushed in and discovered James on the floor. "Oooowwwww!" he howled. He had rolled out of the top bunk and hurt his shoulder.

We trudged downstairs while Dad wrapped him up with an ace bandage. That took until three-thirty.

Before eight the next morning, there was a knock on my door. It was James. "I'd like to go home now," he told me as I gazed at him, bleary-eyed. "My shoulder hurts and I want my father to take me to the hospital."

"Okay," I muttered, tromping down the hallway like a zombie. "Let me call and see if they're awake."

The Hobarts' phone rang and rang, but no one answered. Great, I thought. My brothers have burned their house to the ground, or blown it up, or something worse. I envisioned the phone bleakly ringing in the pile of rubble which once was the Hobart home. "No one's answering," I told James. "Why don't you watch TV for awhile."

Looking put out, James went down to the rec room. On my way back to bed, I met Mathew and Johnny. They'd awakened and discovered that James was missing. "Did James go to the hospital?" Mathew asked me, concerned.

I shook my head. "He's watching TV. Go back to bed."

"We'll watch TV, too," Johnny said, continuing down the stairs. I headed for my bedroom, then thought I'd better watch the boys. The way things were going, one of them was bound to get into some trouble.

I've never been so tired in my life. I was nodding off in the chair when the Hobarts decided they wanted cereal. So I dragged myself to the kitchen and poured them each a bowl of cereal. Honestly, at one point I put my head down on the kitchen table and fell asleep. Johnny, tugging at my pajama sleeve woke me up. "Cereal," he reminded me.

"Right. Cereal," I said as I poured milk into the bowls.

The cereal was greeted with groans of disgust. My mother buys low-fat milk. Apparently Mrs. Hobart uses only whole milk. The bowls of soggy cereal were left uneaten.

Meanwhile, my own family was sound asleep. Usually my household is up and chugging by eight-thirty on a non-school day. Not today. Everyone was exhausted.

At ten, the phone rang. It was Ben. "You're alive!" I said, relieved. "Was it too horrible for words?"

"It was no problem," he said. "They were great."

For a moment I was sure I had fallen asleep at the table again and was having some bizarre dream. "What?" I asked.

"No kidding."

"They didn't destroy your house?"

"No. Mom made a special dinner and we ate it in the dining room. They told my parents about school and the Zuni pen-pal program. Adam talked about the plight of the Zuni people. He was very interesting, really."

"Adam was interesting?" I said in disbelief.

"Yeah. So was Byron. He told us how he came up with the idea to start his own lending library. Then, after supper, Jordan played the piano for us."

"Jordan played the piano!" I shrieked. "Ben, is this a joke?"

"No. Jordan mentioned that he took lessons and Dad asked him to play. He was good."

"I bet Nicky was a terror, though. Right?"

"Nope. Later that evening Dad showed slides of our home in Australia. Nicky was super interested. He asked all sorts of questions. Dad was thrilled with him. Most people yawn through his slide shows. The triplets asked him some good questions, too. Dad was in his glory."

"Ben, did you and my brothers get together and dream all this up? If you're playing some practical joke, I'm going to kill you."

"This is what happened," Ben said, laughing. "Honest."

"Keep going," I said, rolling my eyes to the ceiling. "How was bedtime?"

"No problem. They went right to bed. Then this morning we went downtown for breakfast at Renwick's."

"Oh, that's why you weren't home when I called. I bet that's when your parents saw the real Pike brothers. I hope they didn't have a food fight in Renwick's or anything."

"No. They ordered fruit cups and oatmeal and ate it all. I don't know what you're talking about, Mal. They have very nice manners."

"Good manners? Fruit cups and oatmeal? I'm losing my mind. I can't be hearing this!"

"Is now a good time to drop them home?" Ben asked.

"I guess so," I replied. "Tell your parents James might have to go to the hospital. He may have dislocated his shoulder when he fell out of the top bunk last night."

"Oh, wow! But he's probably all right. James is a big baby when it comes to pain. He always exaggerates."

"He does?"

"Yeah."

"There are so many things I never knew about your brothers," I told him.

"How were they?" asked Ben.

Somehow, I couldn't bear to go into all the details. "They'll tell you about it," I said with a yawn. "See you in a little while."

Still numb with shock, I trudged out of the kitchen and back to the Hobarts. They were busy shooting rubber bands at one another. James had found a way to do it with one hand. Suddenly I wasn't too worried about him.

Not wanting Ben to see me in my pajamas, I went upstairs to get dressed. My bed looked awfully inviting. Vanessa lay snoring lightly in her bed. But I couldn't go back until Ben got here.

As I dressed, I thought about what had happened. It was too weird. It must be something about my house that made boys act zooey. Just like something at the Hobarts' house made boys behave.

Maybe just having so many other kids around made the Hobarts wild. They weren't used to it. Perhaps it was the relaxed atmosphere at my house. There aren't many rules here. The Hobarts probably felt like zoo animals who had suddenly been released. But why had my brothers been such darlings? I guess they just had the sense to put on their company manners. It was more sense than I would have given them credit for having.

Once they were dressed, I rounded up the Hobart boys. I was just helping Johnny tuck in his shirt when the bell rang. "Your brother is here," I told them, surprised to hear how happy my voice sounded.

As we walked down the hall, my mother appeared in the hallway already dressed. She smiled when she saw me. "Rough night with the angels?" she asked.

I just sighed and shook my head wearily.

The triplets and Nicky tumbled into the house, happy and bubbling over with enthusiasm about their night at the Hobarts'.

"Did you have fun?" Ben asked his brothers as he stood waiting for them to pull on their jackets.

"We had a great time," said Mathew. "They have bunk beds and you can do whatever you want here."

"We played lots of games and told ghost stories," Johnny added.

"I hurt my arm," James said sulkily. "But it was okay."

Ben looked at me. "I have a feeling they gave you a hard time," he guessed.

"Let's just say I discovered that they're boys, not angels," I admitted.

"Told you so." Ben laughed.

I waved as they ran down the walk. Then I shut the door and pressed my back against it. "Hey, Mal," said Nicky. "That was a great idea. When are we going to do it again?"

"Never," I told him. "Never. Ever!"

# CHAPTER 14

On Monday I reached gym a few minutes early. Ms. Walden was in her office. "Can I talk to you?" I asked nervously.

She nodded and waved me in. "What's up, Pike?"

Taking my mother's advice, I told her I'd like extra help in volleyball.

"I don't think so," she said. "I don't want to pull a player out of the games at this point."

"Okay," I muttered. Why did I ever think I could talk to Ms. Walden? Feeling foolish, I turned to leave.

"Wait, Pike," she said. "I'm glad you came in because I wanted to talk to you."

"You did?" I asked, worried.

"Yes. I was going to offer you a deal. If you'll play volleyball and try your hardest, I'll ask Mr. De Young to talk to the boys on the other team and ask them to let up on you. I think it's that Brooks kid who's giving you a hard time, isn't it?"

"Kind of." I was surprised — happily surprised. I'd tried to approach Chris Brooks several times in the lunchroom to talk to him, but I couldn't get up the nerve. I didn't know him, and anyway I felt dumb.

"Don't get me wrong," Ms. Walden continued. "Brooks is doing the right thing in terms of the game. He's found the other team's weakest point and he's playing to it. That's good strategy. So we're only asking him to do this as a favor to you." She looked at me and, for a second, her face softened. "It's rough getting clobbered all the time. I can understand that."

"Thanks," I said.

Ms. Walden got up from her chair. It was almost time for class. "I'm meeting you halfway. I expect the same from you," she said.

"Okay," I agreed.

That was how I survived the next four sessions of volleyball. I tried my hardest, as I'd promised, and the other team (especially Chris Brooks) stopped targeting me as their key to easy victory. I did *not* grow to like the game, but I actually returned the ball twice. (Okay, so one time I returned it into the net. The other time I got it to teeter on the top of the net and then fall to the other side. It was something, anyway.)

Then, one glorious day, I arrived at gym to discover that volleyball was over!

"Don't change into your gym suits," Ms. Walden told the class while we were still in the locker room. "We're going outside today to begin the archery unit."

"Swell," I grumbled to Jessi. "Now I don't have to worry about being hit with a ball anymore. I only have to worry about being shot in the heart with an arrow."

Jessi laughed and shook her head. "Hey, I've never done this before, either. I know I'm going to be terrible at it. I don't care, though. It's exciting. It'll make me feel like Robin Hood."

"Boy, you see the bright side of everything," I said as we walked outside to the soccer field.

I was disppointed to find that although volleyball was gone, the boys were not. I didn't even want to think about them armed with bows and arrows. The very idea terrified me.

Ten targets had been set up on the field. Ms. Walden told us to line up in groups of eight in front of each target. Each kid was supposed to shoot six arrows and then hand the bow back to the next kid in line.

After Mr. De Young delivered a big, long lecture about safety, it was time to start. Jessi and I ran to the back of one line together. Ms. Walden gave the command to clear the field (so no one would accidently get shot), and then she gave the command to fire. Arrows flew through the air.

"Look, Mallory," Jessi said as the shooting continued. "Everybody stinks at this. We won't be alone."

She was right. Arrows were flying every-where — and most of them were not hitting the targets. It was a little frightening to see those arrows zooming around every which way.

When the flurry of arrows was over, and Ms. Walden had given the command to cease firing, the few arrows on the targets were mostly on the outer rims. Helen Gallway, who had been first on our line, didn't have a single arrow on the target. "It's nice not to be alone," I agreed with Jessi.

Then Ms. Walden gave the command to re-trieve the arrows. (Everything had to be done by command so that no one was still shooting while someone else was looking for his or her arrows. You can imgine how disastrous that might be!) Retrieving the arrows took forever. The arrows were all over the field. Some ar-rows disappeared altogether. I didn't mind. I was in no hurry for my turn.

A good thing about being last in line is that

you have a chance to see what the other kids are doing before your turn comes. Surprisingly, I discovered I was pretty interested in watching. There *is* something romantic and adventurous about shooting with a bow and arrow. It appealed to the writer in me. (Which is not something I can say about most things we do in gym.)

When Jessi's turn finally came, she shot one arrow squarely onto the target.

Next to her, Robbie Mara couldn't even shoot the arrow. It kept tumbling from his fingers onto the ground. "You're squeezing it too hard," Mr. De Young coached him. "Don't hold the arrow with your fingers. Just let it rest there. Use your fingers as a guide."

It was hard not to smile as that arrow kept tumbling out of his hands. He couldn't get the hang of shooting. What a shame.

From three rows away, I heard Chris Brooks yell. One of the feathers had sliced his left hand as the arrow passed, giving him a sliver of a cut. I know how much paper cuts hurt, so I could sympathize.

"Good luck," said Jessi with a smile when she handed me the bow and the leather arm-guard which protected your arm from the bow string as it snapped back.

The minute I was holding the bow I knew I'd need luck. It was heavy! I strapped on the guard and then loaded the arrow as Ms. Walden had showed us. Like Robbie's, my arrow at first kept popping off, but I loosened my grip as Mr. De Young had suggested and then it was fine.

Standing straight, I aimed and tried to draw back the bow. The string of that bow wasn't going anywhere. It barely drew back a fraction of an inch and I was really pulling. Besides, I needed all my strength just to lift the bow.

I was struggling with this when Ms. Walden approached me with a slim bow made of green plastic. "Try this one, Pike," she said. "It's lighter and has a little more give in the string."

I tried it and the string drew back easily. What a difference!

Ms. Walden gave the command to fire. I pulled back slowly, letting the arrow rest on my fingers, studying the target, trying to keep my arm steady. Zing! The arrow sailed from my bow . . . and flew right over the top of the target.

"You're jerking the bow up at the last second," Ms. Walden remarked. "Either stop doing that, or if you can't, compensate."

The next time I fired, I tried hard not to jerk. The arrow sailed over the top once again. So, the next time, I tried plan B. I compensated. I aimed below the center.

Whap! I hit the top of the target.

"Crook your elbow, don't lock it," said Ms. Walden.

"All right," I replied. This wasn't like volleyball. It was precise and concentrated, and I was in control. And there was something about that soft thud when the arrow hit the target that made me want to hear it again.

With my fourth arrow I aimed further down the target. This time I actually hit one of the colored lines on the top. Arrows five and six clustered by it.

Ms. Walden gave the cease-fire command, and then the retrieve-arrow command. "Nice shooting," she said to me out on the field as I pulled my arrows from the target. "But you're still locking your elbow, and next time compensate even more."

Next to me, Glen Brown pulled one arrow out of the very bottom of the target. "Wow, you got three," he commented, surprised that I had done better than he had. "How'd you do it?"

"Well," I said slyly as I twisted my last arrow out. "It helps if you keep your eyes open."

With that, I ran back to my line. I handed the bow and arrows to Helen Gallway. Ms. Walden advised her to use the heavier bow. "Did you see how Pike drew the bow all the way back under her chin, almost to her ear?"

I heard her coach Helen as I trotted toward the back of the line. "Give it a full stretch like that," she continued.

*All right!* I thought gleefully. Helen had to watch me! What a switch that was.

"Hey! Way to go!" said Jessi when I was standing behind her. "You're a natural at this."

"Not exactly," I said modestly. "I was just lucky. It's not like I hit a bull's-eye or anything."

"Give yourself a break," Jessi scolded cheerfully. "That was the first time you ever shot. You really look confident, like you know what you're doing."

"I do?" I asked, pleased.

"Absolutely. If I didn't know, I'd think you'd done this before."

When my turn came to shoot, I remembered what Ms. Walden said. Concentrating on keeping my elbow bent, I aimed below the target. The arrow hit. So did the next one and the next one. Each time I aimed lower, to compensate for the way I jerked up at the last second. Each arrow hit closer to the center With my sixth arrow I aimed into the dirt.

It hit the bull's-eye!

I'm not kidding. Dead center!

Ms. Walden gave the cease-fire. "Well done, Ms. Pike," she said in front of the whole class.

"It seems a shame to pull it out. Too bad we don't have a camera."

A small ripple of applause rose up. Everyone was looking at me. "Thanks," I said to Ms. Walden, trying not to look too goofy as I stood there smiling.

Class ended before I got to shoot a third time. I was a little disappointed, but glad to end the period with a bull's-eye to my credit.

"Pike," Ms. Walden called to me as we were heading back into the school.

I didn't know what she could possibly want. I hadn't done anything wrong this class.

"Pike, I'd like you to try out for the archery team this Tuesday," she said to me. "You have a lot of potential."

Me? Try out for a team?

"Okay," I said. "I'll try."

For the rest of the day, all I could think about were the archery tryouts. On the one hand it seemed absurd. I didn't belong on a team. Mallory Pike and teams were like oil and water.

But I kept seeing this picture in my head. It was me, standing straight and tall with the bow and arrow in my hand. It looked so right. I really, really wanted to make that team.

# CHAPTER 15

When I arrived at the Monday BSC meeting, Jessi had already filled everyone in on what had happened during gym. "It's Mallory, the huntress!" cried Dawn as I came into the room.

"I don't believe you're trying out for the archery team!" Kristy cried happily. "That is so cool!"

"I probably won't make it," I said. "I just got lucky today."

"Think positively," said Stacey. "You can do it!"

"Sure you can," added Mary Anne.

"Not everybody can hit a bull's-eye," Claudia said. "I can't even hit the target. If you can hit the bull's-eye on your first day, you can definitely make the team."

By the time I left the meeting, my friends had convinced me that there was no way I wouldn't make the team. That night at dinner,

I told my family what had happened. Mom and Dad were just as encouraging. My sisters and even my brothers said they knew I could do it.

The next day, though, I wasn't so sure. I felt a familiar knot in my stomach, the one I get whenever I really want something and I don't think I'm going to get it. So I did what I often do. I told myself I didn't really want it.

I didn't say much at breakfast. I guess everyone could tell I was nervous. They left me alone and no one bugged me about anything.

"You'll do great," said Vanessa.

"No, I won't," I protested. "Maybe I won't even try out."

Mom heard this. "You don't lose anything by trying," she said gently. "Win or lose, we still love you."

I gave her a tense smile and headed for school. Jessi was waiting for me at my locker when I got there. "Today's the big day," she said excitedly.

"Maybe I won't bother. I mean, I have enough to do, with school and baby-sitting and all."

"If I can fit in ballet class, you can fit in archery," Jessi said sternly. "You have to try out."

"Why?"

"Because you like it. And you're good at it. You're just feeling a little scared right now."

When you have a friend who knows you as well as Jessi does, you can't get away with much. "I'll think about it," I told her.

"Think about it while you're trying out," said Jessi.

I felt as if my friends and family had put me in such a position that I had to try out. Either try out, or look like a wimp. I was glad. Otherwise, I might have chickened out.

That afternoon, I did go to the tryouts. Most of the kids there — both boys and girls — were seventh- and eighth-graders. There were only seven other sixth-graders.

The late afternoon had turned cold, and we stood around with our hair blowing and our hands jammed into our pockets. As I waited for my turn, I noticed that the rest of the kids were pretty good, unlike in gym. Most of the arrows hit the targets.

But not one of them hit a bull's-eye.

Unfortunately, I didn't hit one again, either. I did shoot every single arrow into the target, though.

That was good enough. When Ms. Walden read the names of the ten kids who were on the team, my name was among them!

I almost danced off the field, I was so happy. I was heading for home when I heard someone calling me. I turned and saw Ben.

"Hi," he said, catching up to me. "I had a meeting for the school paper again. What are you doing here so late?" Before I could answer, he frowned with concern. "You didn't have detention again, did you?"

"Nope," I said. "I was trying out for the archery team, and I made it!"

"All right! Congratulations!" he cheered.

"Thank you."

We walked home together. I was glad he was there. It's much nicer to be happy with someone than alone. "I guess your brothers better look out now," Ben joked. "They're living with a marksman, or markswoman, I should say."

"That's right!" I laughed.

Ben walked me to my house, and then went back to his. When I opened the door, my house was — as usual — in a state of pandemonium.

Claire was dancing to a music video. Vanessa had spread a zillion magazines across the living room floor because she was making a collage for school. Margo sat beside her building a house of cards.

"Mallory is here!" Margo yelled as I walked in. She jumped up, sending her cards fluttering to the ground. "Did you make the team?" she asked me.

"I made it," I told her happily.

Margo and Vanessa jumped to their feet and ran into the kitchen. "She made it!" I heard Margo yell.

That announcement was followed by the sounds of chairs being pushed around, and dishes banging. I heard my brothers talking. "That's not how you spell it!" said Byron.

"You're putting it on too thick!" cried Jordan.

"Let me do it!" said Adam.

"What's going on?" I asked Claire.

"You'll see," she replied mysteriously.

Now what? I thought. The Pike brothers in the kitchen must mean disaster. I knew I should find out what was going on.

My brothers met me in the doorway before I reached the kitchen. They stood together, with Margo and Vanessa behind them. Jordan was holding the silliest looking chocolate layer cake you ever saw. The right side had collapsed. A lot of the icing had flowed down onto the plate. Written in wobbly letters were the words MALLORY and CONGRADULATIONS!!!!

"Wow! This is great!" I cried.

"The boys made it themselves," Vanessa said. "It was their idea."

"It was?" I asked. The boys nodded. "This is really a surprise. You might even call it a shock. But a good shock. Let's go into the kitchen and have some."

We got out plates and forks and sat around the table. "But what if I hadn't made the team?" I asked as I cut the first piece.

"That's why we were waiting for you to get home," Nicky explained. "If you didn't make the team, we figured you would need a cake to cheer you up."

"Yeah," added Jordan. "We were going to write *Better luck next time*."

"It's a good thing you made the team," Adam said. "Because I don't think we could have fit all that on the cake."

"Well, thanks, you guys. This was really nice of you."

"We know," said Nicky. "We're such great brothers."

We laughed and went on eating the cake (which was pretty good, despite its appearance). It seemed I was going to have to rethink my opinion of my brothers, and boys in general. Even though I'd had a bad run of luck with them lately, maybe they weren't as horrible as I'd thought. In fact, at moments like this, they seemed almost sweet.

With time, maybe they would become angels.

Stranger things have happened.

Look at how I'd changed my opinion of gym. And if that could happen — anything was possible!

## About the Author

ANN M. MARTIN did *a lot* of baby-sitting when she was growing up in Princeton, New Jersey. She is a former editor of books for children, and was graduated from Smith College.

Ms. Martin lives in New York City with her cats, Mouse and Rosie. She likes ice cream and *I Love Lucy*; and she hates to cook.

Ann Martin's Apple Paperbacks include *Yours Turly, Shirley; Ten Kids, No Pets; With You and Without You; Bummer Summer*, and all the other books in the Baby-sitters Club series.

Look for #60

MARY ANNE'S MAKEOVER

As I was brushing Tigger's fur, all I could think about was the BSC meeting. That dumb little incident was still in my mind.

I kept picturing that model with the hairstyle I liked. Stacey had said, "It's not you, Mary Anne."

That's all. Not a terrible insult, right? People say that kind of thing all the time.

But still, it was sticking in my mind like a piece of bubble gum under a tabletop. How could Stacey know what was "me"? Or Claudia, or even Dawn?

I picked up this little hand mirror I have on my desk. Looking into it, I tried to see "me."

I saw a decent, neat-looking girl with sort of blah hair and a gloomy face. I forced a smile, but that made "me" look worse.

Okay, so "me" wasn't so hot. No big deal. Not everyone can be a super-model.

Still, I wondered what everyone found so funny. I reached behind my neck and pulled my hair up. I tried to imagine what the short haircut would look like.

I looked *great* with short hair!

Maybe this really was "me." Maybe all these years I just never allowed the real Mary Anne to come out.

Then it dawned on me. It didn't matter that my friends laughed. *I* laughed when I saw my hair up. A drastic change is always a shock, and maybe shocks make you laugh.

I tried to imagine what they'd all do if I came in with short hair. Sure, they'd probably giggle and make comments at first. But what fun it would be when they realized how nice it looked!

I opened the bottom drawer of my desk, which is my own special hiding place (I got the idea from Claudia). I took out a few fashion magazines I'd stashed there. They were a couple of months old, but I quickly leafed through them.

In the second one, I found the hair cut. Well, not the exact one, but close enough. In fact, this model was a little more my type.

That was when I made my decision. I *was* going to get my hair cut.

#30 *Mary Anne and the Great Romance*
Mary Anne's father and Dawn's mother are getting married!

#31 *Dawn's Wicked Stepsister*
Dawn thought having a stepsister was going to be fun. Was she ever wrong!

#32 *Kristy and the Secret of Susan*
Even Kristy can't learn all of Susan's secrets.

#33 *Claudia and the Great Search*
There are *no* baby pictures of Claudia. Could she have been . . . adopted?!

#34 *Mary Anne and Too Many Boys*
Will a summer romance come between Mary Anne and Logan?

#35 *Stacey and the Mystery of Stoneybrook*
Stacey discovers a *haunted house* in Stoneybrook!

#36 *Jessi's Baby-sitter*
How could Jessi's parents have gotten a *baby-sitter* for her?

#37 *Dawn and the Older Boy*
Will Dawn's heart be broken by an older boy?

#38 *Kristy's Mystery Admirer*
Someone is sending Kristy *love notes*!

#39 *Poor Mallory!*
Mallory's dad has lost his job, but the Pike kids are coming to the rescue!

#40 *Claudia and the Middle School Mystery*
Can the Baby-sitters find out who the cheater is at SMS?

#41 *Mary Anne vs. Logan*
Mary Anne thought she and Logan would be together forever. . . .

#42 *Jessi and the Dance School Phantom*
Someone — or some*thing* — wants Jessi out of the show.

#43 *Stacey's Emergency*
The Baby-sitters are so worried. Something's wrong with Stacey.

#44 *Dawn and the Big Sleepover*
A hundred kids, thirty pizzas — it's Dawn's biggest baby-sitting job ever!

#45 *Kristy and the Baby Parade*
Will the Baby-sitters' float take first prize in the Stoneybrook Baby Parade?

#46 *Mary Anne Misses Logan*
But does Logan miss *her*?

#47 *Mallory on Strike*
Mallory needs a break from baby-sitting — even if it means quitting the club.

#48 *Jessi's Wish*
Jessi makes a very special wish for a little girl with cancer.

#49 *Claudia and the Genius of Elm Street*
Baby-sitting for a seven-year-old genius makes Claudia feel like a world-class dunce.

#50 *Dawn's Big Date*
Will Dawn's date with Logan's cousin be a total disaster?

#51 *Stacey's Ex-Best Friend*
Is Stacey's old friend Laine super mature or just a super snob?

#52 *Mary Anne + 2 Many Babies*
Who ever thought taking care of a bunch of babies could be so much trouble?

144

#53 *Kristy for President*
Can Kristy run the BSC and the whole eighth grade?

#54 *Mallory and the Dream Horse*
Mallory is taking professional riding lessons. It's a dream come true!

#55 *Jessi's Gold Medal*
Jessi's going for the gold in a synchronized swimming competition!

#56 *Keep Out, Claudia!*
Who wouldn't want Claudia for a baby-sitter?

#57 *Dawn Saves the Planet*
Dawn's trying to do a good thing — but she's driving everyone crazy!

#58 *Stacey's Choice*
Stacey's parents are both depending on her. But how can she choose between them . . . again?

#59 *Mallory Hates Boys (and Gym)*
Boys and gym. What a disgusting combination!

#60 *Mary Anne's Makeover*
Everyone loves the new Mary Anne — *except* the BSC!

Super Specials:

# 4 *Baby-sitters' Island Adventure*
Two of the Baby-sitters are shipwrecked!

# 5 *California Girls!*
A winning lottery ticket sends the Baby-sitters to California!

# 6 *New York, New York!*
Bloomingdales, the Hard Rock Cafe — the BSC is going to see it all!

\# 7 *Snowbound*
Stoneybrook gets hit by a major blizzard. Will the Baby-sitters be okay?

\# 8 *The Baby-sitters at Shadow Lake*
Campfires, cute guys, *and* a mystery — the Baby-sitters are in for a week of summer fun!

Mysteries:

\# 3 *Mallory and the Ghost Cat*
Mallory finds a spooky white cat. Could it be a ghost?

#4 *Kristy and the Missing Child*
Kristy organizes a search party to help the police find a missing child.

#5 *Mary Anne and the Secret in the Attic*
Mary Anne discovers a secret about her past and now she's afraid of the future!

#6 *The Mystery at Claudia's House*
Claudia's room has been ransacked! Can the Baby-sitters track down whodunnit?

Special Edition (Readers' Request):

*Logan's Story*
Being a boy baby-sitter isn't easy!

# THE BABY-SITTERS CLUB®

## by Ann M. Martin

| | | | |
|---|---|---|---|
| ❑ MG43388-1 | #1 | Kristy's Great Idea | $3.25 |
| ❑ MG43387-3 | #10 | Logan Likes Mary Anne! | $3.25 |
| ❑ MG43660-0 | #11 | Kristy and the Snobs | $3.25 |
| ❑ MG43721-6 | #12 | Claudia and the New Girl | $3.25 |
| ❑ MG43386-5 | #13 | Good-bye Stacey, Good-bye | $3.25 |
| ❑ MG43385-7 | #14 | Hello, Mallory | $3.25 |
| ❑ MG43717-8 | #15 | Little Miss Stoneybrook...and Dawn | $3.25 |
| ❑ MG44234-1 | #16 | Jessi's Secret Language | $3.25 |
| ❑ MG43659-7 | #17 | Mary Anne's Bad-Luck Mystery | $3.25 |
| ❑ MG43718-6 | #18 | Stacey's Mistake | $3.25 |
| ❑ MG43510-8 | #19 | Claudia and the Bad Joke | $3.25 |
| ❑ MG43722-4 | #20 | Kristy and the Walking Disaster | $3.25 |
| ❑ MG43507-8 | #21 | Mallory and the Trouble with Twins | $3.25 |
| ❑ MG43658-9 | #22 | Jessi Ramsey, Pet-sitter | $3.25 |
| ❑ MG43900-6 | #23 | Dawn on the Coast | $3.25 |
| ❑ MG43506-X | #24 | Kristy and the Mother's Day Surprise | $3.25 |
| ❑ MG43347-4 | #25 | Mary Anne and the Search for Tigger | $3.25 |
| ❑ MG42503-X | #26 | Claudia and the Sad Good-bye | $3.25 |
| ❑ MG42502-1 | #27 | Jessi and the Superbrat | $3.25 |
| ❑ MG42501-3 | #28 | Welcome Back, Stacey! | $3.25 |
| ❑ MG42500-5 | #29 | Mallory and the Mystery Diary | $3.25 |
| ❑ MG42498-X | #30 | Mary Anne and the Great Romance | $3.25 |
| ❑ MG42497-1 | #31 | Dawn's Wicked Stepsister | $3.25 |
| ❑ MG42496-3 | #32 | Kristy and the Secret of Susan | $3.25 |
| ❑ MG42495-5 | #33 | Claudia and the Great Search | $3.25 |
| ❑ MG42494-7 | #34 | Mary Anne and Too Many Boys | $3.25 |
| ❑ MG42508-0 | #35 | Stacey and the Mystery of Stoneybrook | $3.25 |
| ❑ MG43565-5 | #36 | Jessi's Baby-sitter | $3.25 |
| ❑ MG43566-3 | #37 | Dawn and the Older Boy | $3.25 |
| ❑ MG43567-1 | #38 | Kristy's Mystery Admirer | $3.25 |

*More titles...* ▶

## The Baby-sitters Club titles continued...

- ❏ MG43568-X  #39 Poor Mallory!  $3.25
- ❏ MG44082-9  #40 Claudia and the Middle School Mystery  $3.25
- ❏ MG43570-1  #41 Mary Anne Versus Logan  $3.25
- ❏ MG44083-7  #42 Jessi and the Dance School Phantom  $3.25
- ❏ MG43572-8  #43 Stacey's Emergency  $3.25
- ❏ MG43573-6  #44 Dawn and the Big Sleepover  $3.25
- ❏ MG43574-4  #45 Kristy and the Baby Parade  $3.25
- ❏ MG43569-8  #46 Mary Anne Misses Logan  $3.25
- ❏ MG44971-0  #47 Mallory on Strike  $3.25
- ❏ MG43571-X  #48 Jessi's Wish  $3.25
- ❏ MG44970-2  #49 Claudia and the Genius of Elm Street  $3.25
- ❏ MG44969-9  #50 Dawn's Big Date  $3.25
- ❏ MG44968-0  #51 Stacey's Ex-Best Friend  $3.25
- ❏ MG44966-4  #52 Mary Anne + 2 Many Babies  $3.25
- ❏ MG44967-2  #53 Kristy for President  $3.25
- ❏ MG44965-6  #54 Mallory and the Dream Horse  $3.25
- ❏ MG44964-8  #55 Jessi's Gold Medal  $3.25
- ❏ MG45575-3  Logan's Story  Special Edition Readers' Request  $3.25
- ❏ MG44240-6  Baby-sitters on Board!  Super Special #1  $3.50
- ❏ MG44239-2  Baby-sitters' Summer Vacation  Super Special #2  $3.50
- ❏ MG43973-1  Baby-sitters' Winter Vacation  Super Special #3  $3.50
- ❏ MG42493-9  Baby-sitters' Island Adventure  Super Special #4  $3.50
- ❏ MG43575-2  California Girls!  Super Special #5  $3.50
- ❏ MG43576-0  New York, New York!  Super Special #6  $3.50
- ❏ MG44963-X  Snowbound  Super Special #7  $3.50
- ❏ MG44962-X  Baby-sitters at Shadow Lake  Super Special #8  $3.50

**Available wherever you buy books...or use this order form.**

Scholastic Inc., P.O. Box 7502, 2931 E. McCarty Street, Jefferson City, MO 65102

Please send me the books I have checked above. I am enclosing $ _____ (please add $2.00 to cover shipping and handling). Send check or money order - no cash or C.O.D.s please.

Name _____

Address _____

City_____ State/Zip _____

Please allow four to six weeks for delivery. Offer good in the U.S. only. Sorry, mail orders are not available to residents of Canada. Prices subject to change.

BSC1291

Enter **THE BABY-SITTERS CLUB**®

WIN A LOCKET CHARM BRACELET!

# Super Special Trivia Giveaway

10 WINNERS

Take the Baby-sitters Club trivia challenge! Answer all the questions correctly and you have the chance to win a beautiful locket charm bracelet. Just fill in this entry page with the correct answers and return by November 30, 1992.

**15 SECOND PRIZE WINNERS** get Baby-sitters Club portable cassette players!
**25 THIRD PRIZE WINNERS** get Baby-sitters Club carry cassette players!

### Fill in the blanks with the correct baby-sitter's name!

1. She has always lived on Bradford Court. _____
2. She is originally from New York City. _____
3. Baseball is her favorite sport. _____
4. She helped Jackie Rodowsky build a volcano for a science project. _____
5. She burns easily at the beach. _____
6. She has two pierced holes in each ear. _____
7. She would like to be an author. _____

Name_____Age_____

Street_____

City_____State_____Zip_____

Where did you buy this *Baby-sitters Club* book?

☐ Bookstore ☐ Drugstore ☐ Supermarket ☐ Library
☐ Book Club ☐ Book Fair ☐ Other_____ (specify)

BSC192

# COMING NEXT MONTH!

## THE BABY·SITTERS CLUB®

### *Super Special #9*

Opening night jitters, back stage excitement, a chance to be a star! The Baby-sitters are helping out with the big school production of Peter Pan. And with Dawn as Wendy, Logan as a pirate, and Kristy as Peter Pan, the play's sure to be a huge HIT!

**Watch for**
**STARRING**
**THE BABY-SITTERS CLUB!**
**Super Special #9**

Coming in November wherever you buy books!